THE WINCHELSEA RAID 1801

Richard Davis

Dedicated to Eileen Davis 1928 to 2020, a Librarian who loved to read.

CONTENTS

Title Page
Dedication
Chapter 1 — 1
Chapter 2 — 6
Chapter 3 — 9
Chapter 4 — 14
Chapter 5 — 21
Chapter 6 — 26
Chapter 7 — 30
Chapter 8 — 34
Chapter 9 — 43
Chapter 10 — 47
Chapter 11 — 54
Chapter 12 — 57
Chapter 13 — 63
Chapter 14 — 70
Chapter 15 — 75
Chapter 16 — 81
Chapter 17 — 85
Chapter 18 — 90
Chapter 19 — 93

Chapter 20	98
Chapter 21	110
Chapter 22	122
Chapter 23	130
Chapter 24	140
Chapter 25	145
Chapter 26	153
Chapter 27	158
Chapter 28	167
Chapter 29	175
Chapter 30	180
Chapter 31	188
Chapter 32	191

CHAPTER 1

The Lookout Tower

Sun was setting on the newly built Military Canal that had been dug across the Kent and Sussex marshes as a defence against a French invasion. It was a beautiful summer's evening and the cool breeze from the sea rustled through the reeds as we walked towards the town of Rye, but we were late, very late, and so any enjoyment from what should have been a comfortable stroll was lost. My companion in arms, a drunkard called Albert, was late as usual, after his customary and predictable attempt to seduce the barmaid in the New Inn public house at Winchelsea, our home village. Albert failed every evening in this venture through an excess of strong ale and a lack of talent brought on through age; Emma the friendly barmaid knew exactly how much ale Albert could drink before the first repetitions of familiarity and suggestive advances would lead her to switch her attention to other customers. William, the Landlord, sat at the end of the bar each evening with a sly grin watching the Cartwheel pennies held in Albert's purse lighten from his load. Emma was an attractive lady in her late thirties with a mischievous sense of humour and an infectious appealing character; her labours of encouragement would be rewarded later at the Inn's closing with extra tips. William would also make a clumsy advance, as he along with most of the local's found themselves enjoying Emma's company, but he respected Emma as a valued member of staff and friend and wasn't prepared to lose his barmaid asset by compromising her position with an embarrassing approach beyond innocent flirtation.

I reminded Albert of our need for haste, that if the Officer of the watch was at the Martello Tower on our arrival we would be in trouble, not least because our lateness was becoming a regular occurrence. A selection of feeble excuses had been used thus far to one particularly stupid seargent, also on occasion a heavy drinker at the New Inn, who would be fooled by the lame stories that caused our delay but this would not apply to a disciplined Officer of high morals. Albert's walking pace was erratic, he zigzagged and strayed across the pathway that was near the canal and on one occasion stopped with the need to vomit. A friendly face called out offering a lift from a rowing boat on the waterway but this route would take us near the lookout tower front gate and therefore would lead to our detection which in turn would result in the reporting of our lateness. I realised we would need to bypass the soldiers on guard and use the deserted and unmanned rear entrance, we would need to avoid all watching eyes that may inform authorities of our late arrival. I was also doubtful of the rowers' strength to take two passengers in the time frame required and so I politely declined the offer and urged Albert to quicken his pace.

Annoyingly Albert didn't care much about his lookout duty at the Tower or the implications of another late arrival, his attention was taken up by the failed seduction attempt and the need to relieve himself, now three times, of his excesses. Finally the signs and features of the pathway nearing Rye became familiar, we were approaching the Tower where a roadblock and gatehouse was often manned by excitable and youthful trigger-happy recruits. We darted into the bushes and swerved the gate, looking back it appeared unmanned which was fortunate as

Albert by this stage let out a drunken annoying giggle fearing he would fall into the marshy undergrowth. Instinctively I found myself giving assistance and entered the marsh, my two feet now completely sodden adding to my annoyance and the distress of the night watch ahead with soaked feet, there was no apology from Albert who I steadied to continue the walk. We entered the Tower undetected from the secluded side of the rounded brickwork as planned, climbed the rotating stairwell and were relieved to find the lookout benches empty. Rifle muskets, gunpowder and torches had been set out on the table with bread and water rations by the leaving watchmen; they were used to our customary irregular time keeping and had decided not to wait. This would be my station for the next ten hours along with my tiresome companion who had already drifted into a slumber on the internal long bench that hugged the wall. Would that he'd sleep the entire night and leave me in peace with my thoughts!

Why was I here on watch this depressing night? I frustratingly and miserably considered my misfortune. A shortage of soldiers due to other deployments along the coastline and the larger garrison ordered to the narrower English channel area in Kent meant a shortfall in manpower and therefore volunteer militia had been called upon and on occasion coerced into action. Landowners and Gentlemen owners of the farms across the marshes, one of which was mine, had suggested that not volunteering would cause higher rentals. My own relationship with Mr. Watson, who owned my farm, was a complicated and difficult one. He had made a point of saying that the perks I received from him, which apparently included a favourable lower rent, would be stopped, he went further with the threat of blackmail.

"Russell, the storing of Cognac and other goods to the rear of your barn may be found whilst you are away on lookout duty. Don't worry I'll see to it that it won't be detected!!" The contraband and illegal stores belonged to Mr Watson in the first place so he was prepared for the hoard to be found by the authorities, having been heavily depleted in advance by him, if I didn't oblige him with every request. I suspect many of my fellow farmers and friends had his hidden hoards on the land they cared for also, the inference was clear, that it was expected that I and all his tennents sign up to the cause against the possibility and threat of a French invasion.

Mr. Watson's selfish reasoning for initiating a militia army of volunteers came about through aspirations of a heightened reputation amongst his peers, he was a social climber and thought he could better his chances by arranging or coercing the volunteer farming community into action, he had dreams of entering parliament and to meet with Prime Minister Pitt. Albert had also been coerced, not as a farm tenant as he was an odd job man and farm labourer; it had been bluntly stated to him that he would be evicted along with his wife and two daughters from the tithe cottage if he weren't compliant. This threat of eviction was a constant comment made to Albert as he was considered lazy and his work substandard, he was on borrowed time and lived with the continuous warning of becoming homeless along with his long suffering family.

I gazed out over the marshes and further to the sea at the small selection of ships and rowing boats of various sizes in the harbour which at times was a busy sight depending on the political situation between us and France. Now tensions were running higher with the canal completed and a large garrison of soldiers stationed in Hythe, this meant there were fewer ships making their way to the continent and yet some lesser trade still continued. The vessel's before me this evening in the now darkening light were mostly those transporting domestic supplies from the rural farms of south east England along the south coast and to the west of England. The famous Romney sheep were taken to the new world from Southampton and so the smaller boats here held no livestock, only dried goods and fish. Lanterns began to light from the ship's decks and my eyelids narrowed and glazed over from tiredness after the rushed journey here, my drowsiness caused streams of attractive light to beam out in parallel lines across the harbour. My thoughts once again turned to an ever present theme that I was unable to control, now with the solitude of the night watch and the view of the peaceful sea and vanishing sunset, they turned to the issue that had haunted my mind and soul for so long, that of unrequited love!

CHAPTER 2

The Aquilon raiding party

The Aquilon's captain came up from below deck to give the final orders and speech to the assembled raiders who were eager to be underway, they sat excitedly on the benches surrounding the galley floor which was a cramped and dark space. Although it was a short crossing from France, the thirty men gathered used the galley area for their recreation, eating and sleep periods so the atmosphere was oppressive, heavy with the presence of body odour, tobacco smoke and the remains of food platters and empty wine bottles. The character and makeup of the raiding soldiers with poor hygiene and social manners that came from the deprived and criminal underworld, the dregs of humanity, meant that any man of the slightest culture would be desperate to leave the room and the ship's captain was no exception, Captain Courbet spoke quickly so as to not spend too long amongst these men.

"Your orders are simple, be quick once you have reached the three destinations on the coast. Klebert, you'll lead the whole raid but join the rowing team to the extreme right at Winchelsea where there are many cellar properties and so plenty I suspect hidden below. Move quietly across the marshes and through the reeds and once you have arrived use brutal force against all opposition, do not linger unduly, do not set fires as they may attract extra resistance especially the military who we don't know exactly their locations. The objective as usual is to create fear and panic amongst the English, they are the enemy of France, the enemy of our people, our comrades. They meddle and moralise in our freedom and customs, you must view them as your enemy. We are striking at their people to teach them that they can't defend themselves against us or attack our way of life without consequences." The captain left as quickly as he arrived, covering his mouth and nose with a handkerchief and muttering something as he descended to his quarters below.

Klebert grinned at his men in a morale boosting manner of the excitement to come mixed with the contempt they all felt for the officer class and the captain's pretence in social equality and comradeship with the raiders. Klebert's closest allies and friends amongst the group were the brothers, David and Maurice from his hometown of Saumur, the boys were notorious vagrants and thieves who had brought amusement and annoyance in equal measure depending on whether you were a victim or participant in their behaviour. The three men, when in their late teens, had been inspired by the French uprising and, like the Bastille liberating, they joined the violent movement in Saumur that saw many political and social changes over the subsequent years. However there hadn't been a visible improvement in the lives of the people who faced the same problems as before and so the men, like many others, reverted to a life of idleness and criminality but now legitimised by an establishment in turmoil and constant change. Elation, euphoria and hope had been replaced by acceptance and indifference that led to contempt for any supposed authority.

"It's time, let's go!" Klebert roused his men, rose to his feet and patted the men on their backs as they left and boarded the awaiting and already lowered raiding boats from the Aquilon. He shook hands with the two leaders of the other boats and hugged Maurice who was in the Bexhill raiding boat. He smiled at David and the two were the last to board the Winchelsea raid and the three boats soon disappeared from sight of the Aquilon and each other. The fading evening light and slight sea mist made for favourable conditions and they were hopeful that the inhabitants of the south coast would be taken completely by surprise.

CHAPTER 3

Martello

I was startled by Albert who's limbs jumped involuntarily as he drew a deep breath.

"Shit, I feel rough Russell," I poured some water from the jug, a measure into a wooden goblet and handed it over and watched Albert take a noisy gulp. What did any girl see in this heavily tattooed and ill disciplined man I wondered, his boyish charm and gifted easy nature with quick wit had gone, his once colourful stories of conquests from foreign shores were now a bore and heavily distorted from their telling in previous times! Each tattoo that had once been used to ignite the imagination of youthful maidens, of battlefield successes and ship adventures now became filthy smudged reminders of not a glorious past but a fabrication of events. Albert's mind could no longer match the event to the foul ink work. Why was my annoyance and disbelief heightened? I knew the answer but had difficulty in its acceptance. I was in love with his sweet wife, Anna!

It was now dark and Albert had once again succumbed to a state of drunken slumber and Anna returned to my thoughts. I first met Anna when she and Albert moved to Winchelsea with their two young daughters, Mary and Sarah who strongly resemble their mother in looks, nature and mannerisms but not their annoying father. There was an instant attraction for me towards Anna, her first smile in my direction was enough to capture my heart and imagination as it beamed a radiance that held me to the spot. Her body and frame was petite but curvaceous in a healthy way, her hair straight and fair in colour and her manner soft but with a powerful sense of confidence. Her features were not completely even, her eyes wide, alert and of a pale sea blue colour that caught my attention initially the most, it was then further amplified by her wide smile with a slightly larger fuller lower lip. Her teeth were white and even, her skin was smooth and unblemished from the beating sun despite what surely must be some outdoor lifestyle of work. After a fleeting and awkward moment I nervously said hello where we stood in the quiet street that ran between the church and mostly tithe terraced houses opposite, and she replied.

"Hello, my name's Anna, we've moved here" Anna gestured to the house behind her, her two youngsters already excitedly at the door. "My husband, Albert, is with the owner discussing arrangements and work details I think".

I must have stammered, blushed perhaps, released hormones and visible emotions not seen since my teenage years. I clenched my forefinger and thumb together in a grip to bring myself to attention and not disclose my obvious affection.

"That would be Mr Watson, he's a fair man if you keep him happy by staying on his right side. I hope you'll like it here, it's a quiet place mostly".

Anna replied in a strong Irish accent that I was familiar with from a ship's service that I had once done travelling from Liverpool to Belfast. Her accent sounded very out of place here in the Sussex coastal village but added such intrigue to her presence, her nature and my attraction.

"Yes, it appears a lot quieter than we are used to so I hope the young girls won't be too lively!"

"I have two sons myself, slightly older. It's a good place to live," I reassured her whilst not stating my full feelings concerning the landlord. At this point her impatient daughter Mary was calling and with another beaming smile Anna turned away and was gone leaving me with a flutter of excitement in the stomach and the realisation of another excitable problem of life to face. My attraction was not the same as for Emma the barmaid or other maidens from the parish that I had been intimate with on a few occasions before my now happy marriage. This sense I felt for Anna was completely different even from my wife, Caroline, who I believed to be my life partner, friend and confidant. I told myself this attraction to Anna was the biblical "forbidden fruit" temptation that we should not be led into, Pandora's ruinous box and all the rationals that must mean keeping away from her presence in Winchelsea. I wondered whether other men would be attracted to Anna in the same manner, how I would feel if a usurper took my place but I reminded myself continually that neither of us were available to be anything other than neighbours of Winchelsea. Surprisingly there didn't seem to be others that shared my feelings of attraction towards Anna, I would surely have heard any earthy comments of admiration from the locals in the New Inn. I found this startling but reassuring as I would be hurt to hear lured suggestions from the locals or indeed another man who may have feelings towards her!

Primarily I told myself that however tempting to create opportunities and circumstances to meet Anna would lead to embarrassment and most likely humiliation on my part as rejection would surely follow not least due to it being inappropriate. As the months and years passed my emotions of love and yearning grew greater for Anna but I retained my discipline and in doing so became unhappy and depressed. I lost the urge to enjoy life, my family and friends became aware of my mood change and despite frequently asking why, I remained silent as to the cause of my melancholy. Again Albert woke, this time ready for conversation.
"Why do you keep asking about my wife and the children, I don't ask about yours and those sons of yours!"

I didn't reply, I knew there was no need as Albert wasn't really bothered about my inquisitive conversation that in truth was only to inquire into Anna's well-being and happiness.

"I'm going to see Emma again tonight when that damn landlord William is away, I've been watching him and he's often not around in the early evening. Up to no good with that bloody Watson I guess".

I kept silent although I suspect Albert knew exactly what mischief William the New Inn landlord and Mr Watson were up to and I suspected he also knew I was an active player with the use of my farm. Albert's lust for Emma took up most of his thoughts as he continued, "I know your son Robert has been trying with Emma, she's too old for him! Tell him to keep out or there'll be trouble".

"The trouble will be for you, he's fit and rarely in a drunken state like you. If he has fun with Emma I don't mind". I didn't mind, was I a bad father, had I lost my morals, my sense of decency? Robert must learn through life experiences that emotions and experiences, good and bad, are necessary to become well rounded in adulthood. If he succeeded with Emma I knew it would end prematurely because of the age difference and probably with him hurt emotionally. If he failed it would be a slight embarrassment to him but the rejection would help in future advances made to other girls. I wondered how I might feel if Robert's attention was aimed towards another older lady, my Anna. I couldn't countenance the thought and in my heart I told myself that Anna wouldn't find herself in the situation of familiarity with an adolescent and yet why wouldn't Anna be attractive to my son as she is to me and with mutual appeal, if it were not for her being married! I took comfort in the knowledge once more that my son's advances were towards Emma, and not Anna, despite it bringing some displeasure to his mother. My thoughts always returned to Anna, even with the merest of connections to my mundane life, domestic issues and in this instance my son's personal life. Albert sat slouched before me in a semi comatose state and once more I wondered how on earth this idiot could have won her heart and married her?

Our conversation ended abruptly as a large explosion and fire ball reached into the sky to my right side down the coast at what could only be our home village of Winchelsea. Albert bolted up and staggered towards the stone ledge that I was leaning on whilst looking out through the open window and we both saw the orange glow with the church spire lit from beneath. My only thought was of the terrace house opposite the flames that was the home of Anna and her daughters, now young ladies in their late teens. A momentary sense of guilt came over me as I questioned why my thoughts were not of my wife Caroline and sons Robert and Tom but I convinced myself that they were safe. At least they were safe from the explosion as we lived at least two farms away from the parish church of St Thomas that had burst into violent flames. Albert stood next to me startled by the bang and the leaping flames and yet I didn't detect any concern from him towards the welfare of his family, it was as if they weren't his family in the least and this thought for the first time came to me in amazement. I didn't suggest to Albert the possible peril that could lie for those in Winchelsea but instead shook him out of his trancelike stupor glaring gormlessly at the spectacle and ordered him to alert the military garrisoned at Hythe. There was a relatively well rehearsed procedure to alert the inhabitants of the marshes that this could be a French invasion; the first instance was to saddle the horse stabled at the priest's house in Rye and make haste along the coast towards Hythe. I wasn't convinced that Albert understood the order and despite knowing the importance of getting the warning out I knew exactly where I would be running, the five miles along the military canal and towards my home village and what had become my obsessive and love-stricken dreamlike yearning, namely Anna.

CHAPTER 4

The Raid

With a heavy lantern held in one hand and the rifle musket in the other I was unable to run fast but I was making good time in my desperate return home spurred on by the thoughts of distress that could have struck my neighbours, friends and loved ones, of Anna! There hadn't been a French raid for a considerable while but war and conflict was always a real threat since the unrest politically from across the channel and so my heart was pounding with uncontrollable fear. Was Anna alright and her daughters protected? Had Robert returned to the farm where at least I knew Caroline would be safely away from the heart of Winchelsea and the burning church? Would Robert still have been enjoying the evening's entertainment and sport with friends, his visit to the New Inn and Emma? Despite my haste I knew I was at least half an hour away and so I tried to take comfort that in the event of a Raid the orders given to the local community were to scatter inland and either hide on the marshes in small groups or make their way towards the fortification and castle at Bodiam. Perhaps my family and loved ones would have been given enough warning and therefore spared any danger.

❖ ❖ ❖

"Pour quoi diable astu fait ca" Pierre shouted as the flames took hold from the church's porch, Xavier grinned so Pierre asked again in a quieter but more concerned tone, "What the hell did you do that for?"

"Bloody English, it's not my church, they're bloody Protestants!" Xavier's explanation oblivious to the fact that his idiotic act would draw attention from any coastal defence forces nearby. When this was pointed out to the excited and wild Xavier he replied that our work had been done.

"This isn't a full scale invasion, it's a moral booster for us and to spread fear amongst these English idiots. Let's get back to the beach!" Pierre and Xavier were the two Frenchmen nearest the beach and the retreat back home, the other eight men from the raiding party were further into the village enjoying what spoils could be taken from the pub and neighbouring houses many of which had the cellars mentioned by the French naval captain.

Klebert, Francois and David rushed through the New Inn door; the explosion from the church and main street had put fear into some late revellers and Winchelsea locals still discussing Albert's annoying singing of sea shanties and ballads some hours before. Robert saw the glow of the burning church through the Inn window and instinctively and immediately before the intruders entered he bravely pulled Emma towards him and rushed her into the room to the rear, behind the shelves that held the bottles that now violently rattled with the excitable action. William the landlord, an aged and overweight man, had been in a semi state of consciousness due to a lack of sleep and ale and therefore was too slow to escape, he decided to fight the intruders but his decision would prove costly. He lunged towards Klebert with a clenched fist but there was no real prospect of making contact let alone a desissive one that would cause harm. In an instant Klebert had raised his pistol and shot the English "gros vieillard" fat old man in the centre of his face,

William fell to the ground without a gasp or cry of pain such was the accuracy and closeness of the bullet shot. The remaining two locals, twin brothers who also had been drinking to excess, were beaten with single blows about their heads rendering them unconscious for several minutes; they were fortunate to not have been able to show any greater resistance to their French assailants.

Klebert ordered David to search behind the bar and Francois to find anything of worth or interest from the rooms above the pub whilst he searched the body of the landlord for keys, coins and perhaps jewellery. David, a seasoned veteran of French campaigns, had a particular dislike of the English. The English had become to him an object of brutal hatred as he became disillusioned with the dashed hope of the Bastille liberation that he fought so passionately for; the succeeding years had not delivered prosperity for him. Food was not plentiful in France since the regime changed over the subsequent years and as each year passed he needed to fuel his anger. Life was not good for him or in particular his hometown of Saumur where the entire raiding party were garrisoned or lived and for all his gripes and angry venom he had someone to blame, the English were to blame!

David entered the rear room and saw the boy sheltering the rounded figure of a 'spoil of war' and in a call to Klebert he'd decided what action would follow.

"Klebert, there's a lady in here," David shouted to his friend. Robert turned, raising his arm and landed a blow on the upper arm of the intruder, then another punch that sent the Frenchman back by a step but not enough to do harm. Winded but resolute David came forward with a baton raised, there was no need to use his pistol or sword on this boy! But Klebert, already alerted to the excitement in the back room, had entered and decided to kill the adolescent, such was his cold, unfeeling nature that he'd taken his orders literally, "use brutal force on all opposition". Klebert ran his sword through Robert, who was struggling to regain his feet from the baton blow. Robert fell to the ground lifeless, the sword thrust had entered directly into Robert's heart causing instant death.

Klebert immediately looked at the barmaid Emma to see if he felt any sexual urge. He did not and gave David a knowing and disgusting sinister look, was this an endorsement of the wicked act to follow? No, simple indifference as to David's intentions and attitudes towards the English and this poor woman in particular. Klebert returned to the front room of the New Inn and collected the stolen loot his raider colleague, Francois, had gathered from the rooms above and discussed their return to the beach. Looking down the street from the pub window the discussion was also of annoyance that the flames from the church were leaping high into the still dark night sky although the men knew that their departure was fast approaching and with it safety back across the channel, they didn't have long and fortunately for them David came through the door behind with a disgusting grin on his face, an attempt to disguise some embarrassed guilt having satisfied his foul needs.

◆ ◆ ◆

I was now approaching the village and heard rustling in the bushes and reeds around me and the slight whisper of a voice in discomfort, realising that this was likely to be the inhabitants of Winchelsea taking shelter. Before making my way to the burning church for some unexplained reason my instinct was to visit the New Inn, as the pub was the bustling hub of the community this would be where I might find loved ones, Anna and maybe Robert if he was caught in this raid. Robert had certainly been out earlier much to the annoyance of the amorous and hopeful Albert and indeed his mum, the latter wishing he'd spent more time at home studying books and away from youthful antics. Only a French raid could explain the voices I'd heard hiding in the reeds or the explosion from the church as surely gunpowder and anything flammable couldn't be stored in such a sacred place. My panting was heavy, each gasp filled with an excited fear of what lay ahead. Could I realistically be in any condition to raise and fire my weapon accurately, I thought not but would surely try if the invaders were still nearby.

◆ ◆ ◆

Klebert and his unruly mob of companions hurriedly made their way down the street and back towards the beach where the ship's rowing boat, with the fit oarsmen, was waiting to hurry the party back to the awaiting ship, the Aquilon, anchored some way off shore. Suddenly a petite woman who was ushering a younger girl into the small terrace house on the left hand side of the cobbled street startled Klebert. Klebert urged his countrymen on with the order to regroup at the awaiting boats. Why Klebert stopped at that moment of urgency and haste he would never know, what had taken his eye, caught his attention, something worth taking couldn't be the reason. A poor lady in a shabby house of older motherhood age should have been of no temptation! And yet Klebert was held to the spot, he had the sense to send on the raiders saying, "David, I won't be long, wait for me on the beach". The adventurous and dashing commander of the raid changed his direction and rushed towards the front door with a raised boot in pursuit of the lady, with beads of sweat dripping from his forehead and enjoying every moment of his night's work he was genuinely shocked at his impetuous action, action that could put him in heightened danger and certain death he believed if he missed his passage home.

Anna's eldest daughter Mary had made her way up the stairs and into the smallest bedroom urged on by her mother who had seen the men running outside, she convinced herself that with her own older age, in her forties, would save her from unwanted attention but feared for Mary who was exceptionally attractive and had already unwittingly attracted unwanted attention from hopeful suitors. Anna's second daughter Sarah had already managed to make her way to the attic space and was hiding behind a chest and was safe. Klebert burst into the house, kicking open the front door and saw Anna on the third stair in fearful and urgent pursuit of her daughters. When hearing the door crash open behind her and a rusty nail fly loose from the top hinge Anna turned her head to half face her assailant and intruder. Klebert froze, instantly mesmerised by the seductive vision of Anna's back and rear as he viewed her turning frame from her elevated position on the stairs. Her half turned face sent a shiver of excitement down Klebert's spine, it was a face of innocence yet experience, of seductive yet wholesome manner, of intelligence yet naivety. He was full of the excitement fuelled by the raid, the possibility of capture heightened his adrenaline flow but now the vision of Anna filled him with the urge of not just sensual delight but a deeper urge swelling from his heart and gut.

Anna's lower lip had a slight tremble but a defensive action came instinctively to her. In that brief moment of protection for her daughters she held a slight nervous smile towards Klebert and, aware that the man before her was foreign and most likely French she said, and in the French language.
 "S'il te plait je n'ai rien pour toi ici".
Klebert was startled by this, what he had thought was an English peasant, an enemy of everything he stood for and believed since the revolution had surprised him. This woman, so appealing and intriguing, before his leering gaze, in front of him was educated and spoke in a dialect that he didn't recognise as being English and surprisingly in French had said "please, I have nothing here for you". Klebert, whether by reaction or instinct grabbed Anna by the arm and decided that this fair and beautiful woman could not be left and with a tight grip of her

dress and arm he found himself pulling her to his side and into the street. Anna, fearful for her daughter's safety was overjoyed to be leaving them in the house and yet petrified for her own welfare and so was uncertain whether to resist with whatever force she could muster or accept her capture. If she freed herself would this horrible and violent Frenchman return to her house putting her daughters once again in danger? Before long Klebert and his prisoner had passed under the open gated archway and were soon on the shingled beach. Now Anna began to resist but Klebert was a strong man with a powerful grip; Anna soon realised that there was no escape.

CHAPTER 5

The New Inn and aftermath

I reached the pub and hurriedly rushed in unaware as to what I would encounter and yet I had the sense that imminent danger to me had passed, there was an eerie silence other than the muted whimpering of a woman's voice to the rear. The old twins, considered as notable freaks by the regulars, lay by the door with clear bruising and swelling about their faces. Something told me neither brother was dead or in need of immediate medical attention even if I had any doctoring skills, I'd often witnessed a jug of water thrown from the landlord that brought them to the notification of time to awaken and leave so despite their appearance of being badly bruised they seemed as normal to me. My gaze turned to the darkened area further into the pub where I saw the tubby body of William, his face hanging to the right of his shoulder and his almost severed neck drenched in dark thick blood. There was no need or inclination for me to step any closer to William for fear of a sight that would return and haunt my thoughts if I were to do so. Only the parish priest would be of use to poor William!

I cautiously entered the back room and saw Emma with a torn dress sobbing beside the lifeless body of my first born son, Robert. Remarkably and despite his bloody and terrible death his face looking downwards with closed eyes was at peace, the wound to his chest wasn't heavily bloodstained, the wound was oozing blood from his rear and down his back. I leant forward and held my son to my body cradling him as I had so often done in his boyhood when his adventures had led to falls from trees or slipping over when running, I was overwhelmed with grief and heartbreak but managed through a broken voice to speak, "Emma, are you alright, what happened, what can you tell me, who did this?" I realised that my frantic and desperate sobbing questions were too early, that Emma was in shock and from her badly torn dress she had also suffered horribly. However, Emma managed to speak between sharp intakes of breath in broken sentences.

"It was the French…. they spoke French… he was David".

"David, the man who killed Robert?", I asked whilst placing my arm around her shoulders partly to get answers but also in an attempt to comfort.

"No, another man did that, David called him Klebert, I think. It sounded like Klebert". Emma's sobbing grew louder and she became frantic to move away from the lifeless body next to her of Robert. Perhaps she had been more fond of my son than I first thought!

"Emma, walk straight through the pub and outside, wait for help there," I said in as calm a way as I could muster in my grief. I stayed at the side of my son for what felt like an hour, deep in trancelike thoughts of memories, disbelief, despair and anger. As the time passed my thoughts turned to how I would break the tragic news to Caroline, his mother, who by now would surely be frantic with worry and desperately hoping that her son would also be in hiding away from the village. Many of the Winchelsea people, depending on their levels of fitness, by now would be well on their way to the towns of Robertsbridge and Peasmarsh as well as the castle at Bodiam awaiting further instructions and news of whether to return home or in the event of a full invasion keep walking inland.

The long and cold night came to an end as daylight returned to a very different Winchelsea and its people. Some of the locals had returned from their hiding places and those not in a dazed state were dampening down the burning embers of the church leaving an eerie shell-like silhouette highlighted against the morning light. The many surrounding gravestones appeared to have been partly upended in the night's torment, had the resting souls been disturbed by the sacrilege of their disturbed ground. From outside the New Inn I sat in the street, mesmerised by the action around me and the shocked and saddened look of many friends and labourers I'd known since childhood. The damage to St Thomas church was severe, it would take years to rebuild, the stone shell was intact but it now depicted an image that would haunt the community, a reminder of the death and destruction brought to the small farming and fishing village. No one who lived through this night would forget it, from those awfully affected like myself or those who had spent the night shivering in the cold marsh ditches that surrounded the village and its fields.

The empty gatehouse and old mediaeval wall that protected my home of Winchelsea was now an object of annoyance and futile stupidity, if only the soldiers had been here last night! Would they have saved Robert and the landlord or spared Emma her ordeal with some extra warning of the impending danger? Why was I stationed in the Martello tower in Rye with the idiot Albert, who was still absent, last night and not here? I could do no more for Robert, I left him in the New Inn for the local undertaker, bodies were taken to a cold storage resting place before their internment and the funeral service. I began the walk past the now derelict church and back to my farm to look for Caroline. I knew as word got round of relative safety that the remaining people who'd scattered would return, probably by nightfall or the following day. Caroline and Tom I hoped would be waiting at the farm, obviously in a state of worry at the absence of Robert and myself. I rehearsed what I would say to Caroline and how best to tell her with an emphasis on the quickness of Robert's death, a small comfort that he hadn't suffered for long, that the moment of death was so abrupt, that the blade came from a single sharp thrust. I would need to speak with Emma once she had rested sufficiently and agree to a truth that could be told to Caroline and Tom, that the death of Robert was indeed sudden and quick regardless of any other truth. I was sure Emma would give an account centred on kindness towards my wife's feelings.

A young girl's voice stopped me in my tracks as I passed the church, it was Mary who of course I recognised immediately as her manner and looks were so alike to her mother.

"Mr. Russell, have you seen my father?" The girl's voice trembled with fear. I was shocked that anyone would address me as Mr. in front of my first name but I knew it was an attempt to speak with elders respectfully, this was the good manners which Anna had brought up her daughters, both daughters were strong in spirit but grounded in dealing with life's hardships.

"Your father went to Hythe to alert the defences, he should be here soon." In truth I was surprised he'd not already returned, not least because I was aware now of soldiers entering the village from both sides. "What's wrong Mary, can I help?" I asked in fear as I realised that if Mary was in trouble or in need then so might Anna be, my heart began to race, I felt palpitations in my gut and head, I feared the worst from the look on Mary's face.

"It's mum, they took her. I've been hiding with Sarah. It's what mum said to do. Please help."

My emotions were in turmoil, I was on my way to Caroline to break the news of Robert's murder and yet this hammer blow news had rocked me. It felt like I'd been violently kicked in the stomach and yet I stifled my suffering thoughts knowing that they shouldn't be evident to Mary, who knew nothing of my feelings, and was now sobbing before me.

"Don't worry, I'll find your father. I'll look for your mother first who may be at the beach." I urged her to go back inside, stay with

Sarah and wait for me to return.

I ran to the beach and across the shingle now desperately tired from the night's events and yet with renewed energy for a frantic desire and need to find Anna. I feared finding her lifeless body on the shoreline or in the sea, or the image of her sobbing having suffered the same fate as Emma. This would be preferable to the first scenario and I pictured myself giving comfort that could perhaps bring me and Anna to a closeness born from the necessity of comfort, I was desperate to be holding her for my own selfishness before returning her to Mary and Sarah. What wicked thoughts were these I considered, that an opportunity might arise for me to be close, in truth my concern I realised from the past years of infatuation was now deep and true love. My determined effort so far to remain aloof from Anna for the upset and embarrassment that would come from any unnatural impulses could be about to end by circumstances brought about by a French raid.

After a lengthy search of at least a mile of the shingle beach there was no sign of Anna and I fell to the stones and sat trancelike on the shoreline falling into a deep depression of despair, I was ashamed to admit far worse than that earlier felt when I cradled my dead son. Was this now the feeling of a fatal blow compounded by the double tragedy of loss, the first born son and the love I had for the now missing Anna? In the distance and about to disappear, the morning sun caught the sails of the ship that I would come to know was the 'Aquilon'. I knew that my immediate attention and need was to find Caroline but I was pulled in the direction of my heart, a loss of reason and self control and so I made my way back to Mary, Sarah and by their association the pathetic excuse of a husband and father Albert.

CHAPTER 6

Aquilon

Klebert, still tightly holding Anna's arm, threw her on to the long bench that was bolted to the galley wall next to five of the eager and sweaty men that had returned from the raiding parties. Other returning Frenchmen were either on deck or below stairs excitedly discussing their night's actions and adventures which were tinged by the loss of Maurice who they feared was dead. There had been three raids in total, the other two further down the Sussex coast at Bexhill and beyond. All three parties, with varying success from their stealing, scattered the plunder onto the inside wooden decking before them. The plunder mostly made up from the three churches, small manor houses and cellars consisted of golden orbs, sceptres, and pulpit gold edge carvings ripped from their holdings. There was also the loot that had been stolen from private households of hanging meat joints, jarred preserves and in some cases fine linen and clothes. The smaller items of stolen jewellery would be melted down once home and the proceeds shared out once the weight and value had been made.

All French eyes, having first assessed the stolen booty to fuel their expectation and greed, then looked in amazement towards Anna and her being in unnatural surroundings. A mixture of inquisitiveness and enthusiastic arousal came to the still wild and lustful gang. The French naval officer Courbet broke the silence.

"Klebert, who's this? I gave no order to take hostages or prisoners and certainly this thing of no value." Courbet tried to ask in a stern manner but the suggestive grin accompanying his voice gave away his thoughts that the middle aged lady had been brought back for base reasons. As he questioned Klebert he gazed at Anna and instinctively noticed that this was no lady that would usually be known to sailors or those in the military for amusement purposes. He was aware of a look that she had, not classically beautiful but somewhat enchanting! Klebert answered in a defensive tone as he by now had every intention of questioning Anna himself despite the seniority owed to the smartly dressed naval man.

"Captain Courbet, I believe she may be of value, she speaks French."

Courbet was distracted by voices behind him and knew that his responsibility was for the plunder and its value, to keep in check the unruly nature of the French raiders and their thieving manners until an audit had been done. He knew they came from the low criminal classes and was keen for the 'Aquilon' to return to its home port of Roscoff as soon as possible and so turned away from Klebert and the shivering Anna.

David, who by now with his relieved sexual urges following his disgusting actions towards poor Emma had a sense of regret, remorse and self-loathing such was the pitiful nature of the man that before depravity he had no self control but once over felt some return of false self respect. He therefore and unlike the other members of the gang, had less inquisitiveness towards the presence of the shivering and terrified Anna who sat desperately trying to avert eye contact with the rabble of drooling excited men. David looked around him at the shabby party and suddenly realised his brother was absent.

"Where's Maurice?" Anxiously he begged for an answer.

"He was shot, he fell on the beach. I think he's dead" answered Courbet in a distant manner lacking compassion. "His death was reported by the first returning boat so it has been logged officially, I'm sorry". Courbet nodded respectfully towards David in acknowledgment of his loss and left, leaving David to mourn alone, he sat dazed and visibly shaken for at least five minutes and became annoyed at the indifference from his comrades at the death of his brother, the assembled men knew the risks involved and therefore despite being saddened they weren't prepared to ruin the enjoyment of their success and raid. Any sense of remorse and regret David felt for the rape of the lady in the pub had left him, replaced now by an appalling justification that his actions were against an enemy now responsible for his brother Maurice brutal end. David was the foulest of human beings and the weakest of men.

Still other mischievous eyes looked at Anna but the protective body language of Klebert and the raider's tiredness from the night's action meant that Anna was safe. Klebert was keen to question his captive.
"How do you know French, where did you learn it?"
"I was taught by the governess and the priest where I once lived." Anna's French was not completely fluent, it was slow and methodical but she understood enough to ask questions herself. "Why did you take me, bring me here, I have nothing for you!"
Klebert, still shocked to have found a French speaking lady in a coastal village, living as a peasant, questioned further.
"Your accent, your manner, your skin. You are not a coastal English working woman. Where are you from?"
Anna was reluctant at this point to discuss and disclose too much. Although she realised this Frenchman was her best chance of protection against the raiders' lurid stares around her and yet she reminded herself that it was he who had abducted her. At this point the sweaty and unpleasant touch of a raider called Macron made contact on Anna's right side and she instinctively moved an inch or two towards Klebert which

encouraged his urge for more questioning, he gestured for her to speak further.

"I'm from Ireland, I married, and moved away to England. I need to go back to my daughters, I need to go back!"

"You won't see your daughters again, you must accept your surroundings as I do. Get some sleep, you must be tired and you'll be alright here."

Klebert's comment of her immediate safety did not reassure Anna, she was still in a state of shock, of fear and despair and the Frenchmen were still leering suggestively in her direction, however after a while she drifted into a light sleep perhaps through the adrenaline and a biological need to rest the body from its agitated state or perhaps the swell of the sea causing a gentle rocking motion that brought about some sleep. The conditions in the channel favoured the 'Aquilon'; the ship's crew were confident of reaching Roscoff on the Brittany coast by nightfall that day.

CHAPTER 7

Albert's revelation

I entered the village walking up the hill and under the Winchelsea stone walled arch lower gate as before. Once more I thought, what an irony as I looked at the defences built in previous times to defend against a full scale French invasion but useless to the horrible and personally shattering events of the night just gone. As I turned the corner the stark sight of the damaged St Thomas church would be a continual blunt and painful reminder of what had been lost, the object of the French raid to damage English morale and remind the King and governments that they were not to be crossed. The political fallout was of far less significance and damage than the hurt to the locals of Winchelsea, Bexhill and beyond who had suffered the consequences of the conflict more severely than those of differing politics and beliefs. The locals, with their personal memories of the raid, would take much longer for the healing process to take place, if indeed ever.

At the top of the street there was a gathering of the dishevelled, tired and broken folk, their clothes torn, soggy and muddied from the escapes that they had been forced to make, climbing over fences, crossing dykes, and scrambling over the marshy surrounding fields. A small group to the right of this gathering was Mary, Sarah and now with the arrival of Albert. As I approached I could see that Mary, who had an arm around Sarah, was aware that I didn't have good news about their mother.

"I'm sorry, I couldn't find Anna at the beach. Are you sure he took her in that direction?" I gestured as I asked with my head towards the beach. Mary answered whilst holding back more tears.

"Yes, I watched from the upstairs window, they definitely turned the corner and under the arch".

"Then she's been taken to France!" I was genuinely surprised as despite my feelings towards Anna I couldn't understand why in the middle of the chaos of a raid the invaders would take one peasant lady in her middle age. There were other girls of younger age and arguably objects of sexual desire that would appeal ahead of Anna I thought including the friendly and affectionate Emma who I knew they had sadly encountered but not kidnapped. Could it be that the French raid had come specifically for Anna? Could one foul Frenchman have seen in Anna what I had some years before, when she'd smiled at me from this very spot? A shiver went down my spine with the thought of another man lusting or even worse yearning affectionately for Anna. I had accepted any intimacy that she may have had with Albert but through my conversations with him I knew that there was no genuine love. Without love I believed the act of sex was nothing more than a marital ritual sanctioned and encouraged by the church and the established order unless pushed to more excitable extremes from periods of abstinence. Albert being a base and coarse man I'm sure would have discussed his sexual exploits with Anna at the New Inn if they were memorable or indeed even occurred. The male sex to my knowledge and experience weren't in sinc with their female counterparts when it came to the sexual act, I could never understand this, biologically it made sense that a husband and wife's urges should decrease at the same rate. Tales were often told late at night in the New Inn, mostly encouraged by William the landlord and probably to keep the drink flowing, of girls with a lasting and more adventurous sexual urge freely given but in truth I never believed this to be true. It certainly couldn't be true of Anna I told myself, her nature being of gentle purity, and so my sense of fear and worry for her safety was heightened as to the French reasoning in taking her! I didn't convey this alarm to her daughters who stood before me.

"I'm sure your mum will be well, the French wouldn't take her to do her harm. It makes no sense!". I noticed my attempt to assure the girls of their mother and her safety had failed but they smiled and nodded in appreciation of my efforts.

Albert had been standing all this time looking at the church and out to the sea beyond with the same bemusement but lacking the severe heartache felt by his daughters or me. He had the sense however to agree with me and reassure Mary and Sarah that no harm would come to their mother. Mary, to the surprise of me and of mild interest to Albert, said that she heard her mother speaking in French to the man who snatched her and marched her off.

"I don't know what she said but it was French I think, not English!"

"French? You're sure? This could explain the Frenchman's interest in your mother." To my amazement Mary nodded and so I attempted to reassure the girls still further that her mother would come to no harm. We all looked at Albert for if she was a French speaker surely her husband, even the carefree and vacant man in front of us could add more details. He casually began to tell us how he met Anna and what he knew of her foreign language skills.

"Oh yes, she spoke French. We used to joke about it when we first met. It added to the excitement, intrigue and suggestive nature of our encounters in the grounds of the manor. She pretended to be a French maid."

I found it uncomfortable and hurtful to hear of Anna's meeting with this clown but we needed to hear the fuller story and so I urged him to speak further, not least as it became apparent that Mary had no knowledge of it or the history of her parents.

Albert, without emotion and in acceptance of the loss of his wife, continued, "I met her at Divis, the Black mountain, looking down at the city of Belfast. She had a lost expression and so I started to see her. She came back often until we became friendly." He grinned at this point in a distasteful manner. "She told me she wasn't in the employ of the Lord and Manor House but was a sort of 'ward', a family friend rather than a member but in truth, I never really knew! I was captivated and at great risk to my own safety I brought her to England, she stowed away with my help on the clipper."

Before Albert could be questioned more Mr Watson, the overweight and red faced owner of my farm and much of the surrounding land, arrived with news.

"They raided Bexhill also, far worse down there with many casualties. They were taken completely by surprise like us. One Frenchman was injured and caught so we should know more in time!" This was the first and only time Mr Watson had brought good news to me. If the raiders had come with the sole purpose to capture Anna, the French speaking and Irish enigma, living a life in England and hiding, then perhaps the Frenchman held in Bexhill may know more of her being taken. There were some signs of hope!

CHAPTER 8

*The Russell home farm
and Robert's funeral.*

I appreciated the urgency now to find Caroline and my younger son Tom and break the awful sad news of Robert's death. I would try and offer comfort although in truth I knew there was nothing I could do or say other than to impart the truth promptly. I made my way through the village and to the farm about a mile to the north and saw them waiting frantically with worried expressions at the farm house door and seeing my arrival I felt ashamed to have not been here earlier. I'd decided that comfort would come after the news and that my best approach was simply to state the facts.

"Sorry, Robert is dead. Killed by a single blade cut. He didn't suffer, it was instant. He was in the New Inn with Emma." My wife Caroline fell to ground through shock, heartbroken by the news and whilst Tom put his arm around her I repeated the fact that he hadn't suffered, that when I held Robert his facial features were at peace with no visible sign of the violence and anguish of his death. I told Caroline and Tom that I'd been comforted by the knowledge that the small but fatal wound had not outwardly bled onto his body. I also said that Robert had been giving shelter to Emma in an attempt to save her from the assailants; he had died a valiant and brave death with good cause. It was a comfort that he was unaware in his death of what cruelty Emma had endured subsequently.

It was decided by the parish priest and Mr Watson that due to the manpower required for the clear-up operation and rebuilding of the church that the funeral of Robert and William would take place at the same time. The funeral drew a large group of locals who were still desperate for any news or gossip concerning the raid and so the internment took place amongst the whispering and restless shuffling from the congregation. The priest's sermon that accompanied Robert's funeral was the first so there was more respectful attention and concern than for poor William where most of the gathering had lost interest in the priest's utterances of forgiveness and judgement in the life to come. Emma stood beside my son Tom and seemed to show real grief, either from memory of Robert's kindness to her and his failed attempt to protect her, or from a future blossoming relationship that could have formed some deeper romance. My thoughts were of what might have happened had Emma and Robert become lovers or even a married couple, something that would have been frowned upon or even forbidden and yet now in his death we would all have accepted happily, such is the irony of life!. These thoughts made the tragic event much worse, contemplating the loss and waste of life almost became unbearable and yet I stood rigid to the spot and held Caroline's arm throughout.

Robert was buried in a plot next to William, by the side gate that led from the graveyard and into the main street. The congregation left through this gate ahead of me and I looked back at the newly buried mounds, the late afternoon rain hit my face and the church remaining stone shell with missing roof towered above with chard embers and fallen beams still lying amongst the tombstones, the sight was such a depressing and sombre one on this miserable of days! Caroline and I passed in turn through the gate and as if taunting and heightening my sense of grief and emotional loss I was directly opposite the terrace house and the missing front door of where Anna had lived. A deep chilling shiver took hold of my body and I felt my legs weaken and thought I would surely fall, fortunately Caroline gripped my hand sharply and brought me to a state of reality.

"Are you alright, we'll be home soon. You can rest there". Caroline's words added to my sense of shame, as I almost succumbed to telling her of my anguish and the torment I felt about Anna's kidnapping and her well-being.

"Yes, we'll be home soon," I managed to reply but first there was the formality of the gathering in mournful conversation that traditionally and for bizarre reasons follows a funeral party.

Tom I saw walking away back towards the church with Emma, they were consoling each other in conversation and for the first time since Robert's death I entered the New Inn with Caroline. The haunting recollection of William, his head almost decapitated lying in the corner spot by the bar, came to my memory and I shuddered, without asking or thought I walked into the rear enclosed area behind the bottles and after the shock in the outer room my thoughts and memory of Robert's dead body was fortunately more sedate. I was still comforted by the image of his face at peace, uncorrupted by the stupidity of time spent in vice or in disobedience of God's laws, my particular sin so apparent with envy, perhaps lust, that Robert had been spared! The New Inn locals were in attendance as usual and amongst them I heard the loud and at times jocular voice of the idiot Albert. There were also some soldiers passing through, along the defensive lines between Hastings and Folkestone with the main garrison still at Hythe. After any raid regardless of its severity a large number of soldiers were despatched on to the canal, a bizarre show of strength after the event that perhaps comforted some of the farming and local community but to those who had been directly affected by their absence or late arrival caused nothing but anger.

I rejoined Caroline and the others and we each discussed the painful events that still numbed and shocked us, however intertwined in the conversations were reminiscences that brought the occasional half smile and light relief. In the corner three soldiers who had downed several ales were excitedly talking inappropriately in a loud and boisterous manner, annoyingly bearing in mind the many mourners and the sombre occasion. It wasn't possible to ignore the men in their red uniforms with unbuttoned tunics or the muskets leaning against the Inn's front door. It became apparent that they had been at the nearby Bodiam Castle and stood guard whilst a captured enemy raider called 'Maurice' had been questioned. One corpulent soldier spoke loudest and was boastful in his account.

"The Sergeant gave him such a beating but it did the trick," he told the other two who were showing mild interest. "They came from the ship 'Aquilon', the ship is moored in Roscoff and the raiders are from a place called Saumur," laughed the soldier who was evidently proud of his presence at the questioning and torture of the Frenchman. "All sorts of information was gathered but I don't see what use it is, they're long gone apart from poor Maurice who I don't think is much longer for this world!"

I couldn't resist asking this heavy drinker some more questions despite Caroline showing some distress and gesturing with a disapproving look that I shouldn't leave her to do so. I learnt that the soldier's name was Stephen and with the offer of another ale we broke into a separate group.

"Stephen, my son was killed by a Frenchman here, in this very pub, is there anything you can tell me further about these French raiders?"

"No, I don't think so. He said his name, "Maurice", he said he had a brother who was a member of the party that raided here named David!"

"Thanks." I was disappointed not to learn more but also

pleased to have built up a bigger picture of the dreadful night. My aim was to gain as much knowledge as possible. "Did he mention a girl, a lady from here that was of interest to them?"

"No!" Stephen and his comrades departed on their way back to Hythe; they no doubt would visit the hostelries on route at Rye, Lydd and Dymchurch. I doubted they'd be of much use to anyone on arrival. I was fortunate to have gained some information before it had been lost in the drunken memories of these troops.

We each suffered from the grief of Robert's death in varying degrees and in different ways. Tom showed his feelings and hurt in the silent mood that was his nature, a calm and thoughtful boy destined sadly for the life of a farm labourer through lack of education and opportunity. The army or navy was the only option for boys of the parish in search of adventure but Tom's nature would surely prevent this, a fact that Caroline and I were pleased with, more so now that Robert had suffered a violent death. Tom, who had led a sheltered and protected life, many would argue spoiled, would become the support and strength of the family unit. The distractions of friendship with ladies like Emma and the other village girls were still a distant thought and prospect to Tom but we assumed they might come soon once into manhood, but as yet there was no sign. We hoped he would form a friendship that would lead to a successful marriage with the daughter of a fellow farming family but he'd only been close to girls already in relationships and a boy from a neighbouring village from their Sunday schooling.

Caroline's grief was far more severe than I had thought possible, over the ensuing two week period she stopped eating and spent much of her time seated on the ground under a tree of a field on the outskirts of our farm land. At first I left her, believing that solitude and time would bring healing, that she was in her private thoughts and prayers. However after some time and knowing the experience of other villagers who had suffered grief and loss, often brought about through infant mortality, it was advised by the local doctor and priest that work and life distractions were the best cure for melancholy and bereavement, indeed work was the only prevention of falling into an unnatural state of depression that some believed was opening oneself to the devil's prey! Tom, under the instructions of the local doctor, was ordered to forcibly get his mother involved in the farm work that had increased now through the absence of Robert. Robert had always been the brute force needed around the farm; his strength, work ethic and discipline is how the farm succeeded so well. I had spent so long distracted by other duties forced on me by Mr Watson and daydreaming of a life unobtainable that it was Robert who had allowed my failings to go unnoticed! Annoyingly the growing success of our family farm and most of our collective efforts were taken by the landlord, this corrupt and disheartening way of life was, and had been the norm for many generations and would continue we believed for many more to come.

My own grief was more complex, I had been so distracted by the feelings I had for Anna that I'd become distant from the family unit over the previous years, and for this reason I now had shame and guilt mixed with sorrow. Even now when my sole concern should be with consoling Caroline and Tom my mind would continue to wander. Although I had fully understood that convention, duty and God's instruction of how life should be lived, my thoughts had uncontrollably retreated for some time into a fantasy world. I imagined myself living in a bliss like Utopian world with just two people spent hour after hour in a heavenly state, Anna's fair hair falling down around the smooth and unblemished gently tanned petite body. This comatose manner had probably made my friends believe I'd been rendered simple by some unknown accident, I'd been accepted by the people of Winchelsea as a sombre and downhearted character, a person who wouldn't bring cheer or merriment and therefore all conversations I had socially had become brief and to the point.

The locals couldn't detect any excessive outward signs of grief from the bereavement; my downcast manner had become my personality for some time. With the pressures of the farm and the night lookout shifts any extra concern as to my happiness and suffering through Robert's murder or domestic issues had been ignored by others who assumed I was 'soldiering on', only my wife appreciated that there was a deep rooted problem and the change in my character since our first meeting. We were on the surface a happy and settled couple as were so many others who had accepted the life of order, duty and custom after years of marriage. An English country rural parish was littered with examples of unions between man and woman where acceptance of the marital state was the norm regardless of any happiness or even compatibility within the union. Sparsely populated farming communities meant there was a lack of choice in finding a life partner, only issues of shared blood in preceding generations was a factor to decline a marriage, by accident on occasion there were closely related forebears and there were sad and embarrassing offspring results. I'd heard on occasion from sailors and stories in the New Inn of exotic foreign lands where arranged marriages took place with multiple brides, I found this strange if believable. In these parts of England there was no formal arrangement, just an understanding from available parties encouraged by families of the opposite sexes that a union would be good. The system worked well except for those whose habits and mannerisms made them less compatible, like drunken louts who weren't able to appreciate their good fortune! I knew I'd been very fortunate in my marriage to Caroline, it would have been a happy union had it not been for my overactive imagination and the arrival in Winchelsea of Anna. I also knew that only the spark or trauma of an event changes a course in life that leads to divorce, sanctioned by the church and state, or more frequently separation and desertion.

Realistically my only option was to knuckle down once more, accept the loss and murder of my son with little or no resentment, accept my life with Caroline in a very English marriage of aquiescence and embrace the circumstances of my life with stoicism. When people are compelled to either alter direction or make the best of what must be, it still requires courageous action in equal measure of either choice and with Robert's death I faced such a dilemma. I told myself to reluctantly accept the unhappy hand I'd been dealt.

Time went very slowly during the following weeks but Caroline in her very brave, efficient and orderly way made a form of recovery, she spent the daylight hours working on the farm, the kitchen and the house all encouraged by Tom's kind persuasion. Her ability to keep calm in all adversity that befalls a rural community trying to make a living always amazed me and especially now with each day a visible clear improvement in her mood after the tragic loss. And yet awful sad periods remained with evenings being the worst time for us all, I'd been excused from some more night watching duties at the Rye tower although ironically and perhaps typically Albert hadn't been given the same option, I wondered who gave comfort to Mary and Sarah in their loss! I sat restless by the fire most evenings after the nightly chores contemplating my loss, my shattering misery, and festering a hatred of not the French people but those who raided Winchelsea and were responsible for my twofold loss, the deep hurt and realisation of the murder of Robert and a stolen part of my imaginary fantasy of the lost Anna. The thought that I would never see her again, never offer protection if she was in peril and worse of all begin to forget her smile would hurt the most! Shamefully Anna's departure began to occupy my mind far more than Robert's death, I kept this secret from Caroline, Tom and all others. My fear now was that the fantasy world I had been living for so long was coming to a bitter end, the reality was that dear Anna was dying in my imagination, as without her being near and in plain sight, despite being untouchable, there was still a distant hope of her becoming a reality. Now as each moment and day passed she was lost to me and I mourned her absence. I told myself, without belief or conviction, that I must forget her, that this was the turning point in my life, I would spend my time as a devoted husband, father, good farmer and neighbour to the Winchelsea folk and in time I would retrieve a sense of settled happiness.

CHAPTER 9

Emma's pain

Our farm was spread over six large fields where we kept Romney sheep and grew crops, in good times we had a basic standard of living, better than many, for the family and there was the odd perk and gift given by Mr Watson. We knew that we would never become rich from the tenancy but we were conditioned and accepted this rural life. The field at the extreme of our farm bordered the neighbouring land, there was a stream forming a natural boundary, a tranquil and beautiful spot that we often used for relaxation throughout the year. In the summer the sunset to the right changed the colour of the ocean that we could see through the opening tree line. It was a place where passing folk would stop to enjoy the view, the sound of the stream and God's beautiful nature and so we decided to put three strategically placed benches that I'd made from the trees that had previously blocked the sea view. This resting place was adjacent to the main route that entered Winchelsea from the west side and further down the Sussex coast and therefore daily we found ourselves in conversation with travellers, traders and pilgrims on route to Canterbury.

Emma would often sit in this restful setting in contemplation and lamenting her condition perhaps because of the view or perhaps there was a soothing and spiritual significance to the location. She, not surprisingly, didn't find comfort in Winchelsea itself where the Inn was the scene of her attack, or the damaged church which was a scarred and permanent reminder of the horrible and vicious raid. She had worked for some years in the New Inn and was rumoured to be in a loving relationship of William the landlord, the truth behind their relationship was never really known and if there had been tenderness it was more likely to have come from a father daughter type but the rumours continued and were probably fuelled by William with a cheeky grin in the first place. Emma was, despite her worldly experience, a kind and sensitive woman and always aware of other people's feelings. The pub, with a suggestion of ill repute, did no harm to the trade and perhaps encouraged the passing soldiers and those working the canal. Emma had become a seasoned and somewhat hardened asset to the business, she turned a blind eye to any requests made by Mr Watson and William concerning their illegal dealings with the promise of an extra tip, she dealt well by diffusing confrontation with the drunks who on occasion became belligerent and the obvious overtures made by the likes of Albert and others.

She was now however and understandably since the raid a very different woman, having sadly experienced the murder of Robert and the attack on her, her nature and character had changed, she'd lost the bubbly spark of old and became introverted, quiet and sombre. Only when amongst the ladies and girls of Winchelsea did she open up in conversation and appear more relaxed. The exception to this all female party was Tom, seeing them together and occasionally joined by Mary and Sarah, I took comfort in their closeness, perhaps the tragic and desperate group would unite in some healing therapy! Caroline didn't feel inclined to intrude by joining herself, a sense perhaps that she couldn't help them and encouraged me also to not disturb despite their meeting place being on our field, the now familiar resting and recreational spot for villagers and others, how wise Caroline is!

"Robert tried to protect me, I was crouched down and he shielded me. We were rigid with fear held to the spot after hearing the shouts and the bang of the gun. Robert was trembling and could have attempted to exit by smashing the small rear window, why didn't he?" Tears were never far from Emma's eyes and especially now as she told the sad gathering but particularly Robert's brother, Tom.

"He wouldn't want to have left you, he often talked about you Emma," Tom said reassuringly.

"Bloody French, damn them and Klebert the murderer".
Tom, who up till now was unaware of the details of his brother's murderer raised his head that had been tilted in grief.

"What was his name? Was he the man who attacked you?"
Emma was letting down her guard and the emotional hurt was turning to rage as she at times stammered but continued.

"He raped me, his name was David but the other man killed Robert, his name was Klebert. David wore a dirty loose fitting shirt and baggy trousers, he smelt of foul breath, he had many missing teeth."

At this point Sarah was asked by Mary to run an errand; she reminded Sarah that Albert, their father, should be awoken for his food and before his walk to the Rye Martello tower via the Inn. Mary had the calm and reliable ways of the Winchelsea ladies, despite her being still young, she had developed into the role vacated by her mother, an inner strength of optimism and reliability, she had the sense to send Sarah away as the harrowing account could cause emotional turmoil to the very young Sarah. Emma and Tom appreciated the young Sarah being sent off, there was no knowing of where or how graphic Emma's account would lead as she continued having watched Sarah walk away and out of earshot.

"He (David) entered the room and upon seeing Robert protecting me called out to the man, Klebert, who I thought was the leader of the raid as why else would he have been called? He was cold hearted with a determined expression, without any second thoughts he killed Robert with a single thrust. It was awful. His skin was darker in tone and hair colour than the other Frenchman, he was smarter, cleaner in appearance and wore a leather jacket and had a hat hanging loose down his back from the neck."

"This Klebert is the same man who took mum, I was watching from the window, it's the same description. I'm sure of it!" A fearful nervous realisation hit Mary, the thought that the man who took her mother was such a cold, uncaring heartless killer.

CHAPTER 10

Roscoff

Klebert pushed Anna down the steep rope bridge that had been raised for passengers leaving the Aquilon as the French crew stood watching making suggestive remarks and sniggering at the scene.

"Wait here, there's no point running off, you won't escape. There's nowhere for you to run" said Klebert forcibly.

Anna was sensible enough to realise her position was precarious enough for her to see sense and remain as ordered. Klebert was right, there was no chance for immediate escape, however good Anna's knowledge of French and its language was, to try an escape now in a French port far from England would result in failure. She also realised that in Klebert and with the evidence of his protective nature on the Aquilon there was a chance he could be encouraged to release her with the required security. Anna's resolve was to let events run their course in the short term until her own immediate safety was ensured; she knew that Mary would be sensible and keep herself and her sister Sarah safe in Winchelsea, this swayed her decision as despite being desperate to return to her daughters she was not frantic to the degree which would see a dramatic escape attempt lead to certain failure. Mary had been brought up to be assertive when needed, calm in a crisis and make sound judgement when reactions were required; Anna reassured herself that her girls would be well.

Anna stood quietly and wearily watching the action and bustling activity around her, the stolen larger items from the ship's deck were grouped together in sturdy rope netting and then winched and dropped onto the jetty, caught by an army of wiry sweaty French labourers, many wearing the peasant clothing of Culottes and with bare feet. Anna saw Klebert, David and several militia members familiar from the ship disappear into a bar that fronted the jetty with views out to sea. Looking around, she saw an upturned barrel which presumably had been placed purposefully as a brief resting place for the busy labourers. After a short while a large framed and curvaceous lady came from the bar holding a basket and walked directly towards Anna, she was slightly stooped over due to the weight of the basket and in protection against the sea water spray and light rain that swirled about the docks.
"Bonjour madame, je suis Berthe, Klebert m'a envoyé La nourriture et boisson."
"Merci", Anna replied nervously, surprised that Klebert would have been thoughtful enough to send food, as she took the basket. The French maid seemed inquisitive and surprised by the presence of the supposed English lady being brought to Roscoff, there had been many raids but never a kidnapping to her knowledge and if there had been then Anna in no way fitted the imagined type of girl that would be brought back. Anna didn't look to be of childbearing age, which in turn made Berthe assume would decrease the sexual attraction from men's base urges. She decided to remain and watch Anna eat in order to satisfy her inquisitiveness, intrigue and understanding of what special talents or of interest this English captive could have. Berthe slowly studied Anna and from her manners and deportment, realised that this woman was by her nature worldly, sensible, pleasant and with a kind face. This further bemused Berthe, Anna in these surroundings and despite her peasant dress and garb of low class stuck out like a sore thumb!

"What are you doing here, why did they bring you from England?" Berthe asked as she briefly looked back towards the bar entrance, concerned that she might be seen talking with this enemy of France. Anna, whose language skills were sufficiently good enough to understand and speak French when spoken softly and without complex dialects, was able to answer and she welcomed the opportunity to speak freely with another woman.

"Can you speak slowly to me please, my French isn't very good. I don't know why they brought me, I think it was a decision made in the moment by this man, Klebert!" Anna paused slightly but realising that she needed to know as much about her kidnapper spoke on. "Do you know anything about Klerbert, is he a good man, where does he live?"

As the somewhat enchanting captive lady before Berthe had such a pleasing manner it was easy to begin, after the initial hesitation, and enjoy a conversation, with her bright attentive eyes and with a non aggressive petite frame she felt no sense of threat or wrongdoing in answering the questions in full.

"Klebert is like all the others, they're soldiers garrisoned or living in Saumur on the Loire. They come here periodically to leave from the port and return days later with stolen goods of I know not. They normally come home drunk and dizzy with excitement but never with an English man or girl hostage, I can't understand why they brought you."

"I'm not English, I'm Irish." Anna smiled, "have you known Klebert long, is he married?" Anna pressed on with her questions.

"He stays in a room above the bar when here, he's more senior than the others, he's never been bad to me, I don't know if he's married or not, none of them act as if they are! I think he's a good soldier to France and our citizens." Berthe by now had become uneasy at the length of time she had been speaking with Anna, aware of inquisitive and suggestive glares from the working parties around them and gestured to eat the bread and stale pastry from the basket more quickly. Anna obliged and once finished the food kept an earthenware tankard of water, the two ladies parted company, each with a mixture of caution, trepidation and anxiety but they acknowledged each other with a nervous but friendly smile.

Anna now considered her perilous fate whilst looking at the sweaty French labourers and porters on the quay who were busy bringing fresh supplies to the Aquilon, presumably in readiness at short notice to leave port for another raid or a defence action against any English retaliation or aggression. Anna thought once more of her options, would it be a serious possibility worthy of consideration to make an escape here and now, and then attempt to hide somewhere before hoping to rejoin a ship heading back to England, or make her way into the countryside and head north along the coast where she knew there were shorter crossings back across the sea, or hope Klebert could be encouraged and urged by gentle persuasion and reason to aid her return? She shivered at the last but best option and what it might involve, would she have to use her sexual charms to help her cause, the ultimate sacrifice of her body with the pretence of doing it willingly? The thought disgusted her but she was realistic to know that it might be her only choice and plan of attack, however as many, if not all, women know the final act of giving of oneself has to come at the moment of securing victory. Unscrupulous and terrible men could see their victory as a conclusion to their depravity and if not tempted to return, they may refuse to honour their agreed understanding, Anna was sufficiently knowledgeable to know full well how to control this situation should the unpleasant need arise!

At all costs Anna was determined to see her daughters again and soon, her self reasoning and sound mind thought that Klebert was the best hope in doing so. Anna knew that Klebert was a disciplined soldier, came from Saumur and had influence over others. She also knew he was, through his service to France, a devoted supporter of the republic and this was the area that Anna knew most about, her upbringing and education gave her a well grounded knowledge of European culture, history, geography and above all politics. Having come from Ireland and been aware of the French revolt with the Bastille liberation many of her fellow Irish folk and people had looked sympathetically and admiringly upon the French citizens' and the republican cause. Anna spoke and befriended, unbeknownst to the household where she lived, the Belfast intellectuals and intelligentsia in the public library about the rebellion from France and without being personally enthused by the cause, had understood the arguments for and against. This is how Anna would influence Klebert's behaviour, for him to look sympathetically towards her plight but she realised it could be a prolonged and difficult process. Anna had been taught 'oration', 'debate', and acting by reading the Classical Greek authors with their works, plays and morals. She knew she could play any part or role that suited the moment or cause and if Klebert wanted her to be a republican peasant with a gut wrenching hatred of the British with them being the arch enemy of the French people, she could. She could equally play the part of a privileged English descendent landowner having been spoiled and with a disregard for the pain and suffering felt by the impoverished masses.

The rain became heavier so Anna crouched down on the barrel for what seemed to be a long period since Berthe's leaving and so it came as a relief but tinged with nerves when the bar door opened and Klebert appeared.

"Anna, come here." There was no option but to obey and at the doorway Anna was pushed inside the bar, she was instantly hit by the smell and foul atmosphere inside of garlic, cooking oil, tobacco, ale and wine so it was with a sense of fear mixed with relief when Klebert ordered her to the room above the bar which she now knew was called 'Auberge du Quai'. The stairs were old and fragile with many years of use and little or no maintenance, at the top the door to the right was thrown open and Anna pushed inside where the pressure of the shove forced her into a seated position on a single bed. Klebert closed the door behind him and fuelled by the excess of wine from the bar below felt amourous, he sat beside Anna and made, what he believed to be, a polite overture.

"Anna, I must confess that my actions in England were wrong. I'm sorry I shouldn't have brought you here!" Klebert said this and at the same time put his hand on Anna's leg just above the knee so that his intentions were obvious. It was a clumsy attempt at seduction towards a lady of Anna's respectability; his act of verbal contrition in the pursuit of his passion was ridiculous, especially following his forcible opening and bringing of Anna into the upstairs room. Anna wasn't a naive person and knew his hollow apology wasn't sincere, for the first time she realised that Klebert's motives for her kidnapping could simply be of this man's need for base gratification. To have caused so much torment, hurt and wicked harm as to kidnap her filled Anna with disgust and anger and yet she knew that this was not the time to violently confront this pitiful and weak man. In a calm and measured way Anna spoke with her beguiling softly delivered Irish accent.

"I'm here against my will, taken from my daughters, left in the rain, weak and tired from the ship's passage and movement. Please don't!" Anna put her hand on Klebert's upper arm and eased it away from her leg, she became aware of the expression on Klebert's face, a peculiar mixture of regret, remorse, disappointment and anger. Klebert initially thought he'd force a kiss from Anna and brought his face an inch or two nearer but in seeing the reaction from Anna and the slight, almost unnoticeable, quiver in her full lower lip he hesitated and resisted. He decided that his timing was poor, that a seduction couldn't be made under the influence of wine, a better attempt would work but he also knew that at heart he was guilty of a grave crime. The hurt he might cause this captive poor and beautiful and at times timid woman could trouble his soul and conscience, far more than any guilt he may feel for the boy he'd killed from the English Inn or a man killed in war and against a ferocious enemy of the French people. Klebert bowed his head, not quite an apology but a withdrawal and as he left Anna acknowledged his leaving with a quarter smile to suggest she knew Klebert had enough decency to not force himself on her.

"We'll talk more tomorrow", Klebert said and gingerly closed the door as he left. Anna smiled inwardly and with a sigh of relief she thought to herself.

"This stupid man is my passage home!".

CHAPTER 11

Mr Watson's request

Mr Watson often made requests but the tenant farmers and their families all knew that it was, despite the pretence of polite asking, an order. With his obsequious and devoted assistant William, the now former landlord of the New Inn buried next to dear Robert and now dead, there was a vacancy shortage in a trusted ally and accomplice in the shady dealings for Mr Watson to rely on. Therefore just two days after the funerals took place Mr Watson appeared at the farm gates and loitered until he was seen by Tom who notified me of his presence.

"Hello Mr Watson, is there anything you need", I respectfully asked but hoping it was merely a courtesy passing or a quick simple favour.

"Hello Russell, as you know and I'm really grateful I store some items and a few possessions in the out building behind your barn, it's more convenient than my storing at the big house. I have a delivery coming tomorrow and usually William would see it's safely stored but well… you know." Mr Watson paused and stuttered at this moment of awkwardness, he was so selfish that it seemed for the first time the murder of Robert had occurred to him as being killed in the same attack as his deputy and partner in crime. After his pause through insensitivity he composed himself and continued. "I was hoping you'd help out tomorrow, two men will be here an hour before nightfall with a horse and cart, one will stay with the horse whilst the other will need access to the store. If you help him, he'll deposit two boxes and take one from inside. I'll be grateful and see you're alright. You won't be required to do night watchman duties for a while either!"

He noddingly stated my rest from night duty as a clear bribe for my assistance. I had no choice and under the guise of still being in mourning I was able to hide my anger, the fact that I turned a blind eye before made the situation palatable but to now be complicit could have serious ramifications if caught. Mr. Watson repeated his gratitude and tossed over the large key that locked the padlock to the outbuilding. He then briskly walked off towards his Manor House at the edge of the village with a cheery tuneless whistling.

I reported the conversation I'd had with Mr Watson to Caroline and like me she was not happy but realised that there was no option to refuse. As Mr Watson stated, the horse and cart arrived exactly as he said and on time. The Coachman of the cart gazed into the distance with occasional glances up the track in case there was unwelcome attention from neighbours that may have innocently been walking by. A younger man jumped down from the cart and was clearly enjoying his responsibility and the perilous prospects he'd become involved with; his life of criminality gave him a financially more rewarding existence, a life where he clearly enjoyed the degree of danger.

"Hello you must be Russell, best work quickly. You carry this box and I'll get the other. I've been here before, do you have the key?"

"Yes", I said somberly. If I had to be involved in this storing of contraband and a smuggling operation I decided that I should know it's scale and assess, what chances there may be of being caught and if so what the repercussions could be. I knew that criminality on a large scale could lead to deportation to the penal colonies, a lesser sentence was a lengthy period in Newgate prison London. If anyone involved had a loose tongue through excess of ale, or bravado to impress others then I wanted to be forewarned of how serious a crime it could be and so I tried to talk with this young lad.

"You know me by name, what's yours? How long have you been working for Mr Watson? Why are you so cheerful in this caper?" I asked.

"I'm known as Eclair, the name fits my nature, I'm like lightning in my endeavours. I don't work for Mr Watson, he trades with me, it's my French contacts that he needs. War is coming with France so I'm making as much money as I can and as fast as possible. When you start your war with France I'm going back to Corsica where I come from and where I once lived, I can hide there and live out my life happy and wealthy".

Eclair's face was enthusiastic and indeed had a spark of life that I hadn't seen or exhibited for a long time on any fellow man. I was mesmerised by his youth, passion and dreams even if they were on the back of illegal and immoral earnings. It was clear that I liked Eclair very much, he was enjoyable company and I briefly regretted him not being a member of the Winchelsea community and fellow watchman on the long nights in the Rye Martello tower. The time passed quickly as Mr Watson's orders were completed and in a whirlwind I found myself watching the horse and cart leave, Eclair turned from his passenger position and waved and as quickly as they arrived they were gone.

CHAPTER 12

Auberge du Quia bar

A week had passed since the clumsy and obvious sexual overture had been made by Klebert and he'd decided to bide his time and begin a campaign of endearing himself to Anna by what he believed would be traditional methods. As the time passed and there was no sign of a softening in Anna's resistance he became more frustrated and irritated with himself, if only he had built up to the moment of hopeful passion with favours and flattering gestures that had always previously worked. The chase in itself was an enjoyable part of the victory for Klebert from his previous successes but there was something different in Anna, something unexplained, something more than sensual excitement that confused his emotions and upset them in equal measure. Anna was not a French maid and so a different prospect, a different challenge, any outward sign of affection from Klebert towards the lady roomed above the bar would have to be done away from the bawdy drinkers in the bar or fellow militia stationed in Roscoff which was an added problem for Kleberts advances. His every move was being scrutinised and eventually surprised fellow comrades started to question why he had been rebuffed, soon there were open comments and unpleasant conversations with suggestions of better approaches that ranged from the most despicable to downright bizarre.

Klebert had been ordered to wait in Roscoff for instructions as to the possibility of further raids and during this period Anna's presence became widely discussed beyond the confines of the seaside hostelry. Klebert falsely believed that half smiles from random Roscoff folk came about through rumours of his rebuked advances and so he realised that Anna would need to work to prevent further lured questioning and suspicion. Work would deflect attention from the mystery of the Irish lady confined to a small bedroom aloft; the cloak of employment for a working peasant was the best option.

"Anna, can you work in the kitchen, undertake bar service and errands. Please?" He added the word "please" and Anna nodded with a slight smile, she knew very well that this sign of good manners was only added because his intentions were now clear, his plan was to appeal to her decent womanly nature, he would never be polite when giving orders to his military comrades or change his manners towards other women . Better men had tried and failed with false pretence, she thought, and this man's attempt to be polite was clearly out of character, it was ridiculous! Berthe enjoyed the company of another lady in undertaking the toil of the daily chores and the two became firm friends over the period sharing their stories of life's adversity and hardship, they had a great deal in common.

"We start the day with cleaning and tidying the bar area, there's always spilled wine from the night before that needs mopping, then we get the bread from the bakery and start making the Casserole." Berthe's tone was always kind, which Anna appreciated immensely whilst living in the dark and frightening unaccustomed surroundings.

"Why are you so pleasant to me? It must be frustrating and hard for you to talk slowly so I understand your French explaining my duties so patiently."

"I don't see many other women here, my time is spent busy working the bar. Besides you didn't ask to come here, I feel sorry for you. I can tell you are a good person". Berthe gave a look of pity but with genuine affection at this point.

Walking to the bakery each morning the two ladies took the longer route so they could chat and enjoy their time away from the daily toil and the oppressive atmosphere of drunkenness and unpleasant comments and groping from the amorous sailors, militia and dock workers passing through. They often sat in an elevated position looking down at the red tiled rooftops of Roscoff with the busy port adjacent and then the sea into the distance. The ladies wondered what the new world of America was like in the westerly direction; they had heard the stories from the drinkers in the bar of exotic fruits, wild animals, and cultures of men with little understanding but now also the land of opportunity for aspiring folk leaving a warring and impoverished Europe for a more prosperous life.

"I'd like to visit the Americas one day, a fresh start where I'd be accepted and not judged by religious beliefs or my upbringing! What made you live in Roscoff?" Anna said, "I know it's a beautiful place with warm sunshine, picturesque cobbled streets, accessible beaches nearby and fresh sea air but do you like the 'Auberge du Quia' and the people there?"

"I'm not brave enough to leave and I have nowhere to go. My husband died in an accident here in the Port when a rope broke whilst unloading a cargo ship, the load dropped on him. I nursed him but he died a month later. We had a son who died also, of disease so I stayed here with my memories!" Berthe looked pained telling her heartbreaking story but in truth it was a common occurrence, child mortality and accidents around the docks, and she accepted her condition with stoic bravery. Anna held Berthe's hand briefly and they both gazed out to sea in each other's contemplatory and relaxed company.

Each night Klebert spent long hours in the bar considering whether the time had come to make another advance towards Anna, he'd watched her secretively during the day whilst she'd been working with Berthe, there were times he'd seen her at ease and indeed enjoying her labours at the Auberge du Quia and he reassured himself that her new life with him would become a good thing and ultimately bring her happiness. His heart began to yearn for what could be, she would come around, she would accept her position, he would make her forget her old life and somehow he would live with her as his new wife in all but name. There were however a few problems for Klebert to deal with first, he would have to seduce Anna with love and persuasion and not force, he would have to placate her with the promise of reuniting her with her daughters and finally he may need to convince his existing wife who lived in the family house on the Loire river in the town of Saumur to welcome Anna. As Klebert's imagination and fantasising of life with Anna took hold, the acceptance of his wife Lucile to the arrival of Anna would be the easiest part of his plans he told himself, such was the coldness of his heart, a short term annoyance to his wife would be the final act in how events would unfold in his evolving deluded imagination.

It started to notice amongst the tight drinking community of the Roscoff bar that Klebert had deep feelings for this "English girl" that he'd brought back from the last raid. Klebert drank too much wine in the evenings and the conversations began to question why he wasn't upstairs, "braise la fille anglais" he heard often in the bar which led at times to violent altercations. Klebert began to be morose and he began to seriously question whether he'd done the right thing in bringing Anna to France, how could someone so heavenly and beautiful that he'd become infatuated with cause him so much angst, grief and sadness? And yet in the sober light of day and each time he looked upon sweet Anna with her ease and the effect she had on others he was driven on to achieve his ultimate goal of winning her heart.

When the orders came through that there wouldn't be an imminent further raid Klebebert was relieved that his ribbing and listening to foul suggestive comments from his comrades would stop, he also believed that getting Anna away from Roscoff and onto his own territory would aid his seduction. Klebert was concerned to give Anna the news that they were moving on to Saumur; he knew that this would mean Anna being further from her daughters and in doing so cause distress. The right thing to do would be to either arrange to take Anna home to England or leave her in Roscoff where she appeared at times happier in Berthe's company but this would cause him great distress. How could he leave her, be away from her sweet nature, live without her visible presence? He now realised that his willpower to do the right thing was completely lacking and that she would have to accompany him to Saumur. He steeled himself and decided to tell her the following morning.

"I've been ordered to return home and I'm taking you with me. I know you don't want to go but you won't be safe here and I can look after you at my home in Saumur." Anna gave a tearful reply.

"It's too cruel. I have to get back to my daughters, they are vulnerable without me to look after them, they are on their own, they have no one to help them!" She knew that to say Mary would cope very well in her absence and that she had a living partner in her husband Albert, who although couldn't be relied upon, was at least present would put Klebert's mind at ease. She certainly wouldn't mention the existence of Albert to Klebert; this would be counterproductive as she intended to make him believe her affections and heart could be won in the absence of a husband, Klebert must be encouraged in small part, dangled on a string, manipulated to her own ends and news of a husband could compromise and confuse the issue! Klebert was visibly upset by Anna's tearful reaction, a fact that Anna had noticed.

"I'm sorry, I know it's bad news but I will look after you. I think there will be an opportunity for a return to England for you but I don't know when." Klebert had become so torn by his emotions, a growing love for his captive that he wanted to release and his desperate need to have her permanently in his life. Since Klebert's encounter with Anna, entering violently through her front door in the Winchelsea village, his life had

sunk into misery and yet he hung on to the glimmer of hope that he would make Anna happy at all costs. "We are leaving for Saumur tomorrow morning after breakfast, we are travelling by horse and carriage. It's decided."
The time at Auberge du Quia was coming to an end.

CHAPTER 13

A chance meeting with Mary

Mr Watson was now content having believed his labour shortage had been sorted by my forced acceptance into his deeper and more demanding illicit dealings and so he now asked me to return to the night watchman duties when it suited his needs. I left the farm again with enough time for the long walk to the Rye Martello tower although I once again knew that Albert would delay me from his routine of evening ale in the New Inn albeit without Emma's serving from behind the bar. As I walked from home towards the village I was far more depressed than usual, where is the sense in looking out to sea from the town of Rye for a possible invasion when my home is left defenseless, the irony and stupidity of my wasted journey smarted with the absence and murder of my fine son Robert. The damaged and burnt out church of St Thomas on my right hand side was the only remaining evidence of the awful raid but the heartache was stronger than ever. Robert's death was a daily reminder but I knew with the strength of Caroline and Tom combined with the daily grind of work his loss and absence would heal with the passing months and years.

However the healing process and my particular loss I sensed would never happen with the absence and not knowing of

Anna's well-being, it was the thought of her being hurt, in pain, miserable, abused, tormented away from Mary and Sarah that was a permanent pain to me. The pain at times had become unbearable and was damaging to my health. In the past, although I hadn't had many discussions with Anna, we often acknowledged each other with a wave and her heart warming and unforgettable smile sustained my imagination until our next encounter. I now found myself continually telling myself to "pull myself together", I even considered slapping myself forcibly about the face or head butting walls in an act of self harm but I knew nothing would soothe my melancholy state, my sense of loss and my depression that would heighten even more in this first night returning to duty at the tower. This night surely would be a torment not least as I was compelled to spend it with the idiot Albert.

The New Inn was on my left opposite the street that led to the south gated wall into the village and views out to sea. I stopped at this point staring at where Mary, Sarah, Albert and the missing Anna lived and my heart leapt briefly as the front door opened, in the fleeting moment of wistful and excited anticipation I thought I might see Anna coming out. A cruel timing to be pausing at the very moment whilst someone was coming out I thought, how much more misery could be sent down on me I wondered! I saw Mary turn from the door and walk up the street towards the pub with a basket of bread and cheese for Albert's night shift.

"Hello Mary, how are you coping?" I sympathetically asked.

"Sarah and I are well although she's very sad at times. I worry about her the most. I think mum will return one day so we've decided to stay here until she does and be as optimistic as possible."

"If you need anything you must ask, Caroline, Tom and I will do anything you ask." I was beginning to feel uneasy as I was controlling my own emotions speaking to Mary. I felt the need to disclose my own heartache and pain of missing Anna but I resisted this with the thought of it being inappropriate to do so. Mary however became very aware of my hurt and looked visibly stunned, I reassured myself that she must believe my outward sign of grief was to do solely with the pain of my murdered son. Mary was keen to continue our conversation and she knew her father would be in no hurry to leave for Rye, enjoying one last drink!

"My mother wouldn't have been taken in the heat of a quick and dangerous raid to then be killed for amusement. She wasn't the target of the raid I'm sure, despite me knowing nothing of my mum's life before Winchelsea in Belfast, I can't believe a past life of mum's would be of interest to the French. We know this man, Klebert, murdered your son from Emma's testimony and took my mum. Is there nothing that can be done?" Mary's face implored a response from me but I was lost in the moment of longing, my soul tormented by my sense of helplessness. I stuttered, holding back tears of my own, and replied.

"The brother of David who attacked Emma said that they were garrisoned in Saumur, it's inland on the Loire river I think, there's always hope that your mum is there, perhaps working in domestic service."

"So we have a picture of where mum could have been taken, perhaps forced into hard labour or cruelty!" Mary's eyes were now looking to the ground in a thoughtful but saddened state. She paused for a moment and then made further statements that would alter my behaviour, my course of action, my future life! "Mum liked you. She often spoke about you and your kindness, your manners and looks. Is there nothing we can do?" The edges of Mary's lips turned upwards and a sparkle came to her eyes, I was reminded so much of her mother.

Was this young girl teasing me, tempting me, taunting me? I was immediately transfixed, spellbound by the emotional thought that Anna who I'd secretly desired and yearned for over many years may have had genuine warmth and affection for me. My heart beat faster with excitement and I felt my face blush like a teenager in puberty. I didn't want Mary to see me like this with an outward show of aroused emotion but I couldn't help my involuntary reaction. I had the feeling that Mary had intentionally at this timely point set my emotions on fire but if there was a half or slight fraction of a chance that Anna could reciprocate my feelings then I had to do whatever I could to find her, to rescue her, to be with her. Mary either in innocence or, more likely, by purpose couldn't have made her comments without more piercing accuracy or significance and persuasion. I was enchanted, hooked and possessed by a pull to find Anna. I now needed a plan of action.

Albert, having been reminded by fellow drinkers that Mary was outside with his night rations, came from the pub and joined us in the street. Mary passed over the night provisions to Albert and gave me a knowing smile of sadness but mixed with what I thought could be remorseful mischievousness, a knowing smile of her understanding that my thoughts would be excitable and in overdrive throughout the night. I began the walk to Rye in a state of nervous excitement, my mind so possessed by Mary's comments that when Albert spoke I found it hard to answer him.

"Bloody Watson, he's threatened to throw me and the girls out of the house. I suppose Anna kept him happy somehow but now he wants the house for some new errand boy! Bastard." My thoughts were not on his ramblings, not least because his utterances were enhanced yet again by the usual excess of ale, but the suggestion that Anna had swayed Mr Watson to a kind act made my head turn.

"Do you think Anna helped him so that you had a home?" What favours could Anna have done for Watson? I wondered, nothing untoward for sure, she obviously had hidden talents that were becoming more apparent!

"No, but she had this way about her. People naturally helped her, I think Watson knew that Anna would use her power over me to make sure I worked for him without stealing or shirking too much. Bloody Watson!"

"Never mind bloody Watson, your wife's been kidnapped. Aren't you suffering any grief you bloody fool?" I rarely lost my temper so this outburst was met with surprise by Albert. However I controlled my anger and backed down as I knew I would have to spend another ten hours with him in the depressing lookout tower that was looming larger ahead and in sight as we drew nearer.

We reached the tower and found ourselves yet again staring out to sea, on this occasion Albert hadn't drunk the same volume of ale as on our last fateful night together and so was more talkative. The memory of that night and our own helpless situation that saw us uselessly sitting here idle whilst our loved ones were attacked underlined the stupidity once again and the futility of our current nights work. The evening sun faded and the lanterns burned from the boats in Rye harbour as before and we prayed that further raids would target another community than our own, we'd suffered enough! I was aware that Albert also was nervously bemoaning his lot, that his security had been taken with the loss of Anna and that if any harm came to Mary, his responsible elder daughter, he couldn't manage to keep a roof over his head such was his pitiful condition. I decided to probe him further, knowing that information was key in any endeavour and search to find Anna. I also knew that the night would pass much quicker if Albert talked of nothing other than Anna, their meeting, their life together, her habits, traits and mannerisms.

"I've told you most of what I know about Anna. She wanted to leave Ireland and so I helped her. She had some money which we lived on after we got back home but it ran out over time. She refused to ask her family for more, so we live the life of poor English farm workers on the south coast. I'm not sure what she is running away from, only that she would never go back. She refused to tell me so I gave up asking. It must be pretty serious as she lived a wonderful life of privilege in a beautiful Belfast house, her family are big landowners."

"If I made a journey to France in an attempt to find the murderer of my son and to find your wife whom he may still have, would you consider joining me? The Frenchman caught in Bexhill says they came from Saumur on the Loire; perhaps she's there. I want to find the man who killed Robert and…" I paused as I knew that catching this man Klebert, would very much be of secondary importance in my quest and cause but nevertheless I would kill him in a darkly lit place and at a time when he was off guard. Despite my military service from a previous time in my life I wasn't a hardened soldier and I knew I wouldn't confront him in a bout of chivalry one on one. I would slit the man's throat from behind and without remorse I told myself.

"No, she's gone, I must accept it. There was something wild about Anna, she had a nature that couldn't be caged or controlled and I suspect if they got her away on a ship they would have soon found out her true character and thrown her from the ship's deck and overboard before reaching France."

Albert for a moment looked sad but then changed to one of resignation at his wife's disappearance as he said this, his expression then showed it would be a lost cause to even attempt to find her. I hid my dislike of Albert and questioned some more.

"What were her interests, her religion, her political beliefs?" I asked.

"She was clever, very clever. She read pamphlets and papers of all sorts. I don't know what, I can't read myself but one book I recall was by Thomas Paine and other revolutionary writers, she read the Bible to the girls I remember. I think she is Protestant but it wouldn't surprise me if she were Catholic but as I don't know the difference or care it didn't bother me. She could be anything she wants to be!"

I knew Thomas Pain lived near here, further along the Sussex coast and that he inspired the French with his writings amongst others to political activism. I could read unlike Albert but mostly newspapers and issues of local interest, never politics which were of no interest to me. Albert continued.

"She could argue a point from a different perspective from the day before, she was clever. Too clever I used to think, she was taught well in Ireland. She's gone, I must forget her!" With Albert imparting all his knowledge I hoped he'd now sleep and it was by good fortune that he did, he went to his traditional position on the bench and leaning back against the wall closed his eyes and as he did murmured. "Do you think I've got a chance of having Emma now, do you know when she'll be back at work ? With Anna gone I can try my hardest."

The night passed quickly, I was too anxious to rest myself as the thoughts and excitement of my meeting with Mary were whirling around in my mind. Mary's voice was a constant repetition in my brain. "Mum liked you, she often spoke about you…" I spent the night thinking of how I could follow in her footsteps and make my way to Saumur and by morning I'd concocted a risky plan which would involve deceit and danger. The one thing I was certain of was that a return to the farming life and of living in a weak state of acceptance of my loss was not an option. I would either die trying to find Anna or if successful in victory find what I believed could be ecstatic joy.

CHAPTER 14

The long journey to Saumur via Bruz

Berthe and Anna set off for the bakery as was the daily routine but knowing it would be the last time before the journey to Saumur and therefore there was a degree of sadness for the ladies. This morning stroll was the most enjoyable part of Anna's day, a distraction from the anguish of living apart from her daughters and in the unpleasant environment of the rough and rowdy Roscoff bar. Anna, because of her survival instincts from previous experiences, was determined and convinced that at some point she would be reunited with her family back home and discussed this amongst other pleasures with Berthe, who she had become fond of during her short time in the bustling French port.

"I'll be back this way, hopefully soon Berthe and then back home. One option on my return could be to make an escape from Klebert, is there anywhere I can hide near here and would you help me?"

"What good would it do hiding around here Anna, I can't help with getting you back across the sea and I don't see who would. Everyone hates the English and they're unintelligent to understand you are Irish and not an English lady." Berthe extended her arm with a wave highlighting the breadth of the ocean from their usual elevated position where they had paused deep in conversation. Anna smiled.

"I've persuaded a man before to get me across the sea and I can do it again!"

"I think you should be worried and careful saying how you can persuade men, it wasn't that long ago people would say you are possessed by the devil."

Anna in a brief moment of cheerfulness threw her head back and laughed at the thought that the devil had her in his spell, Berthe seeing Anna's reaction smiled which turned into a laugh.

"I'll miss you Anna, I hope you make it back here. Maybe you'll take me to England with you, perhaps the devil will help!" Berthe jokingly said. "Yes, if I can help you I will. There is a disused farm outbuilding nearby, you could wait there until you find passage as a stowaway. But if this were your plan then why not escape now and hide there?" Berthe queried.

"Thank you. If I hide now I suspect there would be an extensive search by Klebert, he wants sex, I suspect more from me, he's obsessed! I've seen it in men before, many men don't know what their emotions tell them, they confuse lust, ownership, control, and think themselves in love. A rare man who loves is the one who controls his own emotions with an understanding of the situation!" Anna frowned at this moment in memory of a man she had known in England. "I must reluctantly travel to Saumur and there somehow get Klebert to bring me back. If I can't, I'll get the devil to strike him down with a lightning bolt ." The two ladies laughed again and walked slowly away in the direction of the bakery.

Klebert was loading a trunk onto the rear of the cart along with some provisions needed for the journey when Anna and Berthe returned, laden down with bread for the bar.

"You can leave us now Berthe, you've got work to do in there," Klebert said to Berthe who was hesitant to leave her friend, she was fearful for Anna's safety despite knowing instinctively that she was by nature a survivor. The ladies embraced each other for the final time and Anna, aware of Berthe's concern, kissed her right cheek and whispered in her ear.

"Don't worry, I've got God and Lucifer to help me!"

The Auberge du Quia door opened and the dirty disheveled figure of David stumbled into the street, he finished his wine and placed the empty bottle on a large barrel on the quay side and wandered towards the cart. Anna was taken by surprise as it hadn't occurred to her that David was also heading to Saumur, at least not travelling with her and Klebert. In truth Klebert was even more irritated at his roguish friend travelling with them; Klebert wouldn't be able to make the flattering comments he'd mentally practised and intended to use on Anna during the journey. He knew it would have been the perfect opportunity to speak with Anna, whilst the coachman of the cart sat at the reins and would be unable to hear due to the noisy wheels and the cart motion.

David's presence would seriously compromise his endeavours or even worse he may introduce into the discussion anecdotes and episodes of events from their previous exploits of rape, plunder and murder when on campaigns or assignments. David's mood was volatile, his senses were inflamed by anger at the English, mourning his brother Maurice, who he strongly suspected was now dead, had deepened his hatred and the merest hint of remorse for the New Inn barmaid he'd raped had now disappeared. Klebert's only hope was that David would spend most of the journey sleeping or in a downbeat and vacant mood but his presence would be unwelcome regardless; he may even become amorous towards Anna as the two men had shared women's company in the past and on occasion in the same evening. If David were to become overly familiar it would quickly lead to confrontation and so Klebert was also guarded and sullen.

With two powerful horses, the coachman and three passengers plus the load, it would take two full days to reach Saumur which was two hundred and fifty miles to the east. The overnight stop splitting the journey was planned to be in the Breton village of Bruz, Anna with a final look back at Roscoff and the sea was thoughtful but determined to return as the cart wheels made their way over the bumpy dirt track and away from the port. The journey started with the hot Brittany sun beating down on the travellers; there was no conversation for the first five miles with only the grunts from David belching out as either rear wheel jolted over a stray stone or small rock. Finally and in a low voice, hoping to keep David out of the conversation, Klebert spoke to Anna.

"Are you alright, we can stop whenever you need a rest."

"I'm alright, tell me about Saumur. What are your plans for me there?" Anna was in a bad mood but not as bad as the one she portrayed to Klebert who was visibly saddened by the hardship that he had imposed on her. Klebert bowed his head sheepishly and momentarily before replying and breathed deeply.

"You'll help out in the kitchen and around the house. It won't be too hard for you!"

David was astounded to hear this degree of kindness towards the girl companion in the rusty and dirty wood panelled seat opposite Klebert, by instinct and without thought he spoke.

"You'll work all day and make love all night!" Immediately David realised his mistake and his face turned pale with fear, Klebert came forward grabbed David by the throat and held his head and upper body over the side of the vehicle which was unnoticed by the driver who sat facing forward urging the horses on, completely unaware of the action behind him. David had witnessed Klebert kill many men in war and peace and more importantly often in a cold dispassionate and indifferent manner. It was therefore with blind panic that David prayed, unable to speak through the tight grip of Klebert's hand, that he wouldn't be pushed over the side of the cart causing death or almost certain severe injury. For David it appeared to take a long while as he pleaded with Klebert in head gestures not to be dispatched, he looked down in fear at the dry dusty soil rushing past his head just feet away. Klebert said nothing but brought the trembling David back to his seat, leaving David gasping for breath, he would avoid all eye contact for the next two days until reaching Saumur.

Had Klebert spared David for the sake of the girl who he began to feel a genuine love for? To murder or harm David at this point wouldn't further his interests or endear her to favour him had she witnessed such a cold brutal attack. It was against his better judgement not to inflict more pain on David, he felt wretched for showing weakness and leniency and thought that he may live to regret his decision not to be rid of the trembling and pathetic David! Klebert had no idea of how Anna was affected by David's crude comments or his violent reaction to them. The truth was that Anna, who obviously showed alarm and unease that affected her own safety as the confrontation unfolded in front of her, was indifferent to David's physical pain but Klebert didn't know this or anything about the character or temperament of his captive. Some women who befriended the lowly military type were excited by the danger of a liaison with a man of violence; perhaps many believed themselves to be more protected and secure in their presence. Other ladies were disgusted by gratuitous violence but in truth and on this occasion Klebert was totally out of his depth and realised the extent he would need to go in understanding Anna's nature if he was to win her heart.

"You'll simply do kitchen work until I've thought of what to do. I'll show you Saumur, you'll be alright." Klebert said softly in an attempt to reassure Anna, the rest of the journey to Bruz was in silence from all parties.

CHAPTER 15

Another favour for Mr Watson

The morning sun rose over the horizon, I could hear the murmuring of soldiers and the workers of Rye stirring and looking down from the tower and from our vantage point I could see the day relief soldiers mustering. This was our permission to leave the watchtower and make the journey back towards Winchelsea and home. I made an excuse to Albert, in order to not make the return journey with him, saying that I needed to return as soon as possible. I had nothing more to learn or gain from him with regard to Anna and their previously shared history and so I walked alone with my thoughts. How would I convince Caroline that I intended to travel, at great personal risk, to France? I certainly couldn't tell her the truth, in that the main reason was I am, and have been for a long time, in love with Anna and I can't live knowing that she is in harm's way. Arriving back in Winchelsea I passed the New Inn on my right hand side, I could never view this oak beamed Tudor building in the same light as before the attack. It had been a place of such good times, especially at Harvest when the entire village met inside and around the surrounding streets for an abundance of ale and other delights. Passing further and on my left was the now haunting sight of the church frame and looking down from the stone walled graveyard I could see straight through the missing front doors, down the nave and at the large cross behind the altar. A shiver of guilt for misplaced grief ran down my spine, a sense of impending danger, a harbinger of doom, of a reminder or instruction to change from my destructive course. I knew from pulpit sermons that to desert my wife, my son and my responsibilities today and especially so soon after the murder of Robert was wrong in God's eyes. I paused for a moment staring at the church. Would the cold light of day, the morning clean fresh air, the stark view of the headstone of my murdered son Robert buried before me bring me to my senses? No, Mary's comment was embedded in my mind, "mum liked you." The merest of hope would direct me uncontrollably onwards!

I was almost at the farm gate and tethered there was the horse that I knew to be owned by Mr Watson. I sighed heavily knowing that there was another request for help, that yet again one that couldn't be refused, another order shrouded by the threat of blackmail and sure enough he appeared from behind a tree.
  "I have a delivery tonight so I'll square it with the 'watch' that I need you for farm work at home. It will be the same man as before, arriving at dusk. Is this alright?" Once again I couldn't refuse.
  "Yes, where did you meet Eclair? He's an interesting man!" I wanted to know more about Eclair and unbeknown to Mr Watson I was looking forward to seeing the young man with Corsica connections once more. He would be a moment's light relief in a seemingly long period of misery.
  "Don't concern yourself too much with that man, you don't need to know much about him or his business. All I'd say is desperate men are dangerous so be careful." Mr Watson's warning I suspected was to protect his own business dealings with Eclair and not my personal danger in befriending him but I took the warning as to cease asking questions.
  "How is Caroline and your other boy doing? I am sorry about the raid, I think war is coming with France and then they'll all

pay for it!"

"They're doing well, they work hard and time is a healer." My reply was quick and to the point as I suspect Mr Watson's concern wasn't too heartfelt.

"War will come, the information I'm hearing from London and the troops at Hythe is that there is a build up for invasion. I must be on my way." I watched him leave, I turned and walked through the farm gate for a day's rest before my second meeting with Eclair, the Corsican.

Sure enough at dusk the cheerful young man was driven up to the gate by the depressing and downcast figure of the quiet coachman who was slumped over at the helm tightly holding the reins.

"Good evening Russell. I heard about the Raid, you didn't say your son was murdered the last time we met. I'm sorry." Eclair attempted to speak in a more sombre manner; however he was unable to change his natural upbeat and optimistic personality or mood as he dismounted from the cart. I considered this not as a failing but a strength in Eclair, if anyone else had offered commiserations in such a light hearted manner I'd have seen it as an offence, maybe sarcasm or an attempt to be harsh but I had no doubt as to this Corsicans intentions.

"It was truly awful, we are suffering badly." After a pause and a few deep breaths I continued. "I saw him, at the pub, soon after the attack and he looked at peace. The witness there, a girl, said he didn't suffer for too long, it's a comfort for my wife. We must learn to live with our loss although I naturally want revenge!"
We unloaded the boxes from the cart and stored them as we had on the previous occasion in the outbuilding and said nothing, Eclair was sensitive to my feelings and the grief I was suffering. As we stacked the last box I felt the need to talk further with Eclair, I had the sense that he was a man who could be trusted, confided in and possibly one I could ask for assistance.

"Have you got time for a drink, a conversation in private away from your coachman and friend?" I gestured towards the cloaked man who sat stationary, his head turned away and staring out to sea.

"Yes, absolutely. Never mind about him, he doesn't even speak English!"

"There's benches at the end of this field and a flagon of ale I placed there earlier. Shall we…"

We walked across the field after Eclair spoke briefly in French to the coachman whilst patting the horse, we soon found ourselves seated and enjoying the drink that I'd intended to consume alone, but now happy and comfortable sharing in this man's company.

"If I wanted to get to France, how easy do you think it would be? I'm thinking of going as there's a faint chance I might be able to find and kill the man who attacked Robert, my son."

I knew it was risky to confide in Eclair but I didn't trust Mr Watson or his warning concerning Eclair, besides the man before me, in the failing daylight, gave a sense of honesty and reassurance. Eclair at this direct question looked startled, I think he was very surprised by the thought that I was capable of murder even when fuelled by rage and revenge.

"I can get you to France but your quest must be as you say in English, 'like looking at a needle in a haystack". He laughed at this point, reflecting on his poor English although I suspect he must have known that his mastery of my language was very good! "Tell me your plan once in France." Eclair's eyes twinkled in excitement.

"We know that the man who killed Robert was named Klebert, that he has a comrade called David who raped the barmaid Emma, that the two men are garrisoned in Saumur on the Loire river, that they came and returned on the ship Aquilon for the raid and that with all this information there is a remote chance I can find them." Eclair, having considered the facts, was doubtful that armed with this knowledge alone the venture would be successful.

"It still sounds very unlikely that you'll find them." Eclair's scepticism was understandable but I continued.

"I also suspect Klebert is travelling with a girl named Anna who he kidnapped from the village here and so I have a description of him from the girl's daughter who witnessed the kidnap. He has dark features from possible Moorish ancestors, tall, and slim in build."

Did I blush, surely he would not have noticed in this darkness at the mention of Anna and her kidnap, something in my tone, my voice and conversation must have alerted Eclair, he smiled and immediately spoke with a grin.

"You like this girl, you want to find her?"

There was no point in hiding my feelings and emotions from Eclair, I trusted him sufficiently to know there was no gain to him in knowing my private thoughts, he wouldn't speak to others about them. I also knew that if I was going to be helped by him I'd need to be honest and give him all the information I had.

"Her name is Anna, she lives in Winchelsea with her husband, or partner, and their two daughters. I've admired her from a distance for many years but recently have become more attracted to her. I think love, I know it's love! And now she has gone, I can't think of anything else, I feel driven by an uncontrollable passion and need to find her, to know she is well and perhaps rescue her. Maybe I'll die in my attempt but I must try." Eclair looked at me with genuine concern.

"Love shouldn't cause such upset and harm. I've seen men and women ruined by love but I've learnt enough to know that it must run its course even to the disaster that usually follows! My advice is to grieve for your son with your wife and forget Anna but I know you won't. I can help you get to France and advise on travel once there but do you have support here for your search?" Eclair had found the flaw in any French adventure and rescue attempt; he knew full well, as did I, that I had no backing from my wife, my family, friends or most importantly the landlord of the farm, Mr Watson. I knew that to discuss any plans with them would never be supported, moreover it would meet with vehement opposition, anger and suspicious hostility.

If I were absent from the farm it is certain that Mr Watson would evict Caroline and Tom and find another tenant farmer within a short while such was my dilemma and the high risk stakes involved.

"Do you have any suggestions, Eclair, on how I can get support or help here?" I asked the young Corsican as we finished the ale and he rose to his feet preparing to leave.

"I'll give it some thought and call by again, but next time unbeknown to Watson. I can tell you that you'll need to act fast as the trail may run cold and even if she's made it to Saumur this Anna could arouse suspicion and be in danger. So you must be decisive and above all else act before war comes, it will be soon." I knew how important it was to act but hadn't yet considered the stark and cold reality that Anna would be held captive in a country that we would be at war with, despite her knowledge of the French language, her Irish or British accent would give away her foreign nationality. My expression must have been mournful which was detected by Eclair and in his normal cheerful way he made his farewell.

"Keep as cheerful as you can, Russell, it could all turn out well. I have a feeling that our interests might be mutually aligned, say nothing yet to your Caroline and I'll see you again soon."

Eclair mounted the cart and after giving instructions to the mysterious coachman he departed, this time it was too dark to see him wave but the lantern from the cart gradually disappeared having passed the bend in the track that passed our farm.

CHAPTER 16

Bruz and the journey to Saumur

Bruz is a quiet town with a population of two thousand people that mostly work in the surrounding rural farms or are in the service of those passing to and from the Brittany ports. The two Inns with rooms of varying sizes and stables kept busy with a steady flow of tradesmen, military and merchants all making their way to and from the coast. Klebert, and his passengers, arrived and he was shown to the room that faced the busy street of passing trade. Anna was ushered up the stairs, which raised no eyebrows or humour from the Innkeeper or customers who were loitering in the lobby area, the Inn was often used for fornication, dalliances and prostitution and despite Anna's appearance being not of an obvious prostitute, dressed to excite or arouse suspicion, it was assumed she was. David had been told to sleep in the small bedded area adjacent to the stabled horses, he was still sheepish and smarting after his chastising and altercation earlier and therefore with some inferior red wine he was content to accept his squalid surroundings for the night.

The room allocated to Klebert, who was a regular traveller passing through, had one bed with a dirty mattress, one wash basin, and one chair placed by the window.

"You take the bed Anna, I'll sleep here looking out to the street so you'll keep your dignity and modesty. I won't watch you undress however tempted I may be!"
Klebert instantly regretted the cringeworthy latter part of his comment, and looked to the floor, at what he considered must have been and sounded like another clumsy and inappropriate attempt to show some affection towards Anna, this time by displaying respect for her privacy but ruining the sentiment by the 'temptation' remark. He wondered how, with his confidence and usual sexual approaches now completely lost to him, he'd ever manage to impress Anna. In this lady's company he had become like a fourteen year old virgin, babbling with insecurity and an innocence not felt since the awkwardness of youth. Klebert turned to the window and thoughtfully observed the street activity regretting once again his inappropriate advances and stupidity.

Anna realised that the failure of Klebert's clumsy attempt had further emboldened her and so, with the advantage in the moment, decided to play for attention and get some growing sympathy towards her cause. Knowing that the young Klebert was an active supporter and participant of the 1789 revolt, she decided to tell a story that would gain her empathy and some pity, which in turn may arouse remorse for her position leading to a hoped-for passage home.

"I've slept in worse rooms than this and on filthy flea ridden mattresses before when we were enslaved by the English as a family in Ireland. They forced my parents into hard labour and put me to work when I was old enough in the Manor kitchens. I won't need you to teach me anything about cooking and kitchen work, I've been enslaved before!"
Klebert felt a piercing blow of guilt in the pit of his stomach, a deep sense of the hurt he'd caused to the beautiful Anna which now was deepened by the knowledge of her hardship of life's previous experiences. He decided to end the conversation abruptly as he became aware that to hear further from Anna

would cause himself deeper sorrow and the real possibility of breaking down before Anna's eyes. It would be an awful display of weakness, of manhood and of self worth to the once proud soldier.

"I'm sorry you've had a hard life, I think you should get some sleep now. Life won't be bad for you in Saumur."

After an hour Anna was asleep, her breathing had become a little louder and deeper. Klebert gently and silently rose from his chair and stood above the sleeping Anna gazing at her face and body in the candlelight, he was mesmerised by her natural beauty, womanhood and yet innocence, he had an overwhelming pang of growing love which caused pain knowing the circumstances of their meeting and his behaviour. So great was the pain that Klebert believed in that moment that he feared a gasp of despair would come from his mouth and gut and awaken the poor sleeping Anna. He returned in silence to the chair by the window and spent the night awake, unable to sleep and feeling wretched for his Winchelsea behaviour, if only he'd been in the other raids further to the west, if only he had never met Anna, he thought. And yet if man is destined through life to find and meet one true love, and if Anna was the one, which was the growing belief in his heart, then what cruelty of fete had allowed the circumstances of their meeting to happen in the way it had? Klebert pondered his Winchelsea actions, should he have left poor Anna with a vow to return, should he have attempted to remain at the small terrace house in the height of the raid and state his love? Ridiculous, Klebert shook himself to reason, he wasn't in love at first sight, he would have been killed as an enemy of England, as was the man and boy in the public house being enemies of France. Klebert was in mental torment, going continually over in his head the occurrences bringing him to this desperate state of near madness.

Dawn came and Klebert gently stirred Anna from her sleep.

"We'll have breakfast and then set off. We should reach Saumur by nightfall if we travel well and in good time. I know I was wrong to take you from your home, I'm not sure why I did. Can we at least be friendly to each other until I work out the best course of action so you can see your daughters again?"

Anna sat up from the bed and gave Klebert a look that showed acknowledgment of his sentiment of remorse but was mixed with a hint of displeasure, of hurt and of fear that was intended to make Klebert compound his deep regret. The expression of Anna's was timely and well delivered causing maximum hurt so there would be no light relief in the second day's journey that would see them reach Saumur.

CHAPTER 17

Eclair's return visit

I sat in the small kitchen area of our farmhouse with Caroline having finished our evening dinner. It had now been weeks since the awful events of the raid that had brought such harrowing sadness to us, beyond that which anyone could envisage in similar circumstances and yet the inner strength of Caroline with Tom's assistance proved that the hardship and hurt could be endured. I had mentally conditioned myself to the loss of my first born child and fed my melancholy with a mix of senses, one of anger that would be satisfied by revenge with the murder of a Frenchman known to me only as Klebert and one of future hope satisfied with the rescue and saving of Anna. The latter I knew would bring misery to Caroline if my fantasy of a successful attempt would also bring the romance I secretly hoped for with Anna, it was an issue I put to the back of my mind as I was realistic enough to know the likelihood of success in my intended and risky quest was very unlikely.

Outside I could see through the square panelled window that the sunset was turning the colour of the trees to an orange glow, it had become my custom each evening around this time to take my flagon of ale and make my way to the benches where I'd sit for a while looking out across the English Channel towards

France and to where my lost Anna may be. The strong ale helped to bring momentary comfort to my troubled state of mind but later I would regret its consumption when waking in a more distressed state than had I remained sober. I was reminded by Caroline and the recollections of her previous mourning behaviour that this self absorbed unhappy state was not good, that my mood wasn't improved by contemplation looking towards the disappearing and symbolic sunset of remorseful regret. She advised me that in the summer months watching the sunrise would make more sense but it had become an evening ritual. With the beer in hand I reached the farmhouse kitchen door and was pleasantly surprised to hear a now familiar voice.

"Hey Russell, are you there?" said Eclair.

"Evening Eclair, good to see you. Shall we speak at the benches as before or inside?" I asked despite knowing that our conversation wasn't for Caroline, after a brief, courteous and polite acknowledgement between Eclair and Caroline we made our way to the corner of the field and sat once again with ale looking out to sea through the purpose-made gap between the trees.

"War is coming, Napoleon is on the warpath with the Kingdom of Great Britain, Prussia, Austria and it would seem everyone else. He's trying to form an alliance with Spain but regardless of this there will be war soon. Therefore my time in travelling, whilst not completely free at the moment, will become impossible and I'll lose important contacts. My business in your cold and heartless dreary country is coming to an end!" Eclair was serious in his account but with the same air of optimism, he was a believer in that when circumstances change then opportunities arise. "In light of this need for action I have a plan and I would like your help which will enable you to travel through France, get your girl and return home or follow me to Corsica. I won't make a judgement on your decision!"

The thought of living in blissful happiness with Anna filled me with excitement but also shame, and embarrassment. Although I was a friend and confidant of the contraband smuggler before me I wasn't yet happy discussing a subject that I knew was morally wrong and would cause such harm to Caroline and Tom. I also knew that a life with Anna in Corsica would be out of the question, in the unlikely event I could kill Klebert, rescue Anna and announce my undying love I knew that regardless of her feelings she would first want to return to her daughters. I decided to stick to the issue immediately in hand and not of the interesting consequences or prospects further ahead, besides which, it would be tempting fate to consider dilemmas following a dreamlike outcome. I first had to be successful in the dangerous and risky quest and at this point I reflected on my stupidity in thinking there was any chance of success!

"What's the plan?" I politely asked, leaning forward, out of habit to hear something away from prying ears, despite being completely alone although within view of the Coachman still patiently waiting.

"I supply three farms along this coastline with French Brandy, amongst other stolen items, that are stored in outbuildings such as yours. I'm paid in coins, some gold with both British Guineas and French Livres and I know where the money is kept by Mr Watson and the two other landowners. I have a large delivery arranged for all three sites next week and as it's my last visit to England with war coming, I intend to rob all three before making my escape by the usual route across the marshes at Dungeness. I'll take from each location and in addition have the allocation that is intended for each. I've arranged to sell the whole lot to a man I know from Lewes down the coast and the two lads who work for him and are from Cranbrook to the north, they'll meet us here late at night and pay us in gold. You see that man, the Coachman?"

"Yes", I nodded attentively.

"He's French, speaks no English, he watches my moves and makes sure I don't steal or fiddle with the French suppliers that he works for on the Calais side of the channel. We'll need to kill him, I'll then need your help so you'll take his place and help me row back to the waiting boat off the coast. Whilst we're taking the gold coins and money here at your farm I'll give the impression to your wife Caroline that you are being forced at gunpoint and that I'll hurt you and your other son, you'll have no choice but to assist! If you are successful and return here, either alone or not you'll be able to blame your capture on me and make some concocted story of events. Once in France I have a plan before meeting up with connections there and with gold coins in hand we can travel fast southwards, I'll drop you off at Angers on the Loire and then continue south to Marseilles before Corsica and my life of luxury."

Eclair excitedly looked at me for a reaction and an answer. I paused for a minute, thought of the plan which gave me the option of returning by blaming Eclair and appreciated that this plan was my best chance of success. However my reluctance came from the thought of us killing the quiet Frenchman driving the horse and carriage, I also knew I'd need funds for my own journey in France.
  "If I were not involved would you still kill this man without me and how do you intend to do it? I'll also need some help with money to get to Saumur and then make my return."
I think Eclair felt slightly saddened, maybe let down by my lack of enthusiasm but he answered with the same optimism.
  "I'll let him, the Coachman, know you are a friend, he trusts me. After we've taken the gold he'll be pulling the small boat from its anchorage on the marshes, we normally drink a nip of Brandy before rowing out, I'll come up behind him and strike the bottle over his head, then you'll hold him beneath the water until dead. I'll give you some of the money, just enough to help you reach Saumur and help with your return."
Once more Eclair stared at me for an answer, he appeared to be looking deep into my soul as his plan involved deceit and emotional turmoil to Caroline and Tom but now compelled with the awful sin of murder. What wicked ideas had possession of

my mind, my judgement and nature, my love and need to find Anna surely wouldn't sink to these mortal sins and depths! Something though told me to agree, I told myself that when the time came I would find an excuse to not murder an innocent, to prevent such a crime but in this instant I found myself agreeing to the plan. Had I become obsessed in this pursuit of madness? Would Anna look favourably on an obsessed mad man, a murderer?

"I agree," I found myself saying.

"Good, then I'll see you once more to finalise arrangements before next week and then it's to France and with God or the devil's luck we'll live or die!" Eclair laughed and was gone with his final gulp of the warm ale.

"Goodbye Russell, until next time."

CHAPTER 18

Saumur

The horses and carriage approached the crowded and bustling town of Saumur from the north of the Loire river, Anna looked cautiously from her seated position towards the row of houses that faced the river, ahead was the main bridge of two hundred metres that spanned the flowing water. Further up the river was a smaller crossing used mainly by pedestrians and all around there was a hive of bustling and hectic activity that Anna hadn't seen or experienced since her life in Belfast many years before. Many of the features of her once home town were similar to that of Saumur, both having a large basilica and church, a thriving community of trade and industry. As the carriage crossed the bridge there were tradesmen pulling carts on the right hand side, groups of three or four gathered gazing out over the river Loire as it widened and meandered into the distance. Anna, considering her situation, still nervous and missing her home, was however impressed by the view, the cobbled streets and the architectural beauty of Saumur was stunning and attractive in its own and unique way. It was a bright late summer day that added to the attraction and because Anna had an immediate sense of her own security by instinct and witness to some irrational but now thoughtful behaviour of Klebert, she felt a sense of calm.

Klebert, with a nod of his head made eye contact with Anna and spoke whilst pointing into the heart of the town.

"I live in that direction, we turn left here. You'll wash clothes over on the north bank, across that footbridge. The market is in the opposite direction, on the right, on the south side near the church, you'll visit there each morning for bread and the day's meat and fish order. I'll escort you around tomorrow, I know you speak good French but please realise there is no chance of escape from here and despite the port of Angers down there you won't find boats sailing out to sea going to England." Klebert's tone was direct as he knew that soon arriving at his home he would need the pretence in front of his wife Lucille to explain Anna's presence as nothing more than an extra maid in the kitchen, a gift from England! Despite being master in his own house and imposing his will he was in no mood to initiate on arrival an explanation or argument with his wife by saying that he'd been enchanted by an Irish girl that he had intended to capture and enslave for sexual gratification, but through a deepening respect bordering on infatuation and love couldn't bare to do her harm by forcing himself on her. No husband, however brutally honest, would be so open with a wife and especially as his initial intentions towards Anna had failed which in turn had led to a warped sense of failed manhood.

At the foot of the bridge on the south side David alighted with a miserable grunt, Klebert saying he would meet up with him on the following day in the Rue St Nicklaus where there were many bars, drinking houses and brothels frequented by the military personnel of the garrison. The carriage travelled up the cobblestone street named 'Rue Bouju' until coming to a halt outside a town house that belonged to the Klebert household.

"Here we are. It's getting late so I'll see you tomorrow and you'll meet Lucille who manages the house. We have a maid, Frances, who sleeps in a room next to the kitchen. You'll have to sleep with her tonight and we'll sort out something better for you tomorrow."

Anna once more found herself being held by the arm and ushered towards another bedroom, this time one shared by a servant. In passing, Anna reminded Klebert of her past experience.

"I remember your enemy and mine, the English, doing this to me once!"

Klebert, unable to speak any more to Anna or give any form of comfort, closed the door behind Anna and spoke with Frances in the hallway outside, his next challenge would now come, speaking and explaining the presence of Anna to Lucille who would surely, from experience of her husband's previous unscrupulous behaviour, be furious.

CHAPTER 19

A conversation with Caroline

I spent the following day mulling over in my mind the discussion I had agreed with Eclair and considering the merits and failings of his plan, unfortunately in the absence of the necessary funds and knowledge required to travel through France and reach Saumur I knew that if I were to attempt a rescue of Anna this was my only option. The problem causing me the most serious grief was the murder of the Frenchman that Eclair so casually mentioned in the cold hearted manner. I'd shot at men before with a musket and on one occasion bayoneted an enemy combatant but never in cold blood murdered an unarmed man. I intended to kill Klebert who would preferably be unarmed at the time giving me the advantage, I had justification for this planned action but this was not the case for Eclair's colleague who was unknown to me. I considered Eclair's plan, that he would strike the Coachman from behind and across the back of his head with a full bottle of brandy and that this indeed could do the job of murder, leaving it unnecessary for me to drown him in the watery marshes. I put the thought to the back of my mind and imagined how I would deal with the immediate issue of informing Caroline of my intentions, my plan to find and kill Klebert.

Caroline and Tom, like me, had suffered dreadfully by the heartache felt through the murder of Robert. Eclair's plan, that would give the impression of a forced kidnap at gunpoint into aiding his theft and then my disappearing, I knew would compound and cause further misery, torment and grief. I knew this would be unfair, cowardly and cruel and so I had ruled out this plan of deception towards my wife. I had however decided that it would be the account that Caroline and Tom should report back to Mr Watson and the military personnel stationed along the canal defences; it was, after all, a good plan. It was the only plan! It meant a difficult conversation with Caroline, one that for obvious reasons would not involve any mention of Anna. My deceit and ruse in explaining to her would be that the sole reason for my French voyage would be of revenge and justice for Robert, I doubted Caroline would think that an attempt to find Klebert would succeed, to kill him even more unlikely and in truth I suspected that she was right.

"Caroline, I need to speak with you. Can we go for a walk, perhaps down to the beach? It's important." It was mid afternoon and there was still work to do on the farm so my request came as a surprise to Caroline who was keen to start the evening meal of broth and potatoes but she nodded with a slight look of alarm. We strolled out through the farm entrance and towards Winchelsea, from the Main Street under the stone arch gatehouse once more and towards the shingled beach.

"I know what I'm about to ask will be a surprise to you, especially as you know my character and nature isn't a violent or aggressive one. I know you'll advise against it and I know that everything you say, every reason you give, every argument you give me will be the correct one and that my head tells me I'm going to do the wrong thing."

We stopped on the shingle, the tide was going out and there was a calm and beautiful blue sea beyond the thin strip of sand, a cool sea breeze was calming the tension that I'd created by forewarning Caroline of what I was about to say. Caroline looked at me with concern as I continued. "We know a great deal about the man who killed Robert, his name, his appearance, his companion the rapist and most importantly where he is garrisoned with his army colleagues. I've spoken to Eclair who has a good plan to help me find Robert's murderer and get our revenge. I intend to find him and kill him and return as quickly as possible." Caroline's response came as no surprise.

"You're not serious, it's ridiculous. Even if you find him, he won't be alone, I've seen this small framed man Eclair on the farm, will he help you kill him?"

"No. I must do that alone. I wouldn't expect help from anyone to do it, but I will. I'll slit his throat from behind, I don't intend to duel with the man. He gave Robert no chance and I won't give him one either!"

"So what happens here whilst you're away playing stupid games, you can't bring Robert back. Why do such a stupid thing, risking your own life and leaving me a widow and Tom without a father. What happens to us?" Caroline's questions, as I suspected, were well reasoned and made such good sense but by now I was focused on the plan and how it would unfold.

"The plan is that you'll see and witness me being forced at gunpoint or blackmail, threatening danger to you or more likely Tom, to assist Eclair in the theft of gold and Cognac hidden at our farm and two others nearby. You'll report back to Mr Watson that I had no option other than to assist and therefore he'll be sympathetic and allow you and Tom to manage the farm until I return, it may only take a month. I haven't told Eclair that you know the plan, he thinks you will genuinely believe I've been forced and we are in danger but we've been through so much, and I can't allow you to suffer more grief." Caroline bowed her head and sobbed, filling me with such pity and shame for my silly and foolhardy intentions. I was also ashamed not to mention that finding Anna was secretly my main obsessive reason for the dangerous undertaking and yet what would be the point in mentioning Anna now or indeed at all? If I were successful then Anna's return would arguably be to the life she had as before with her idiot partner, why should I assume that the rescue of her would bring about some affection towards me? I would return to being the kind farmer who once committed a heroic act of revenge and that by coincidence brought about the return of a 'farmhand's woman'. In the passage of time my courage would be forgotten but at least my life would return to the one that included Anna albeit from afar, where I could be reassured in the knowledge that she lived safely and from a distance I could admire her once again as before.

In this moment of stark reality with my wife in tears I thought about my intended actions. I doubted the outcome and consequences once again, would the plan be futile and pointless as Anna may be dead, thrown from the Aquilon on route back to France as predicted by her heartless husband. If I were to find her would she be no less attracted to me upon her Winchelsea return, would I be seen as a pitiful overly romantic fool if my unrequited love were discovered by the community at large, would I become the village idiot or in my own despair become the village drunk, what embarrassment would poor Caroline suffer as a consequence? Would the ultimate embarrassment come from being laughed at and regarded as a fool by Albert? My mind and thoughts were in a state of flux and yet I kept my composure before my wife with no intention of discussing Anna, she may already be dead I repeated to myself and if this were the case then it would be even more evidence of the stupidity of my actions, what a fool I had become. If only Mary hadn't spoken to me about her mother!

Caroline raised her head.
 "Is there nothing I can say to make you change your mind?"
I remained focused and calm and replied in an attempt to be reassuring to Caroline but also myself.
 "No, the plan is well made and it's the only chance of success. Eclair says there will be war soon with us and France so he's not

coming back, he knows France well, he has connections and will get me to the Loire, from there I'll reach Saumur. Soldiers drink in bars, I don't think it will take long to locate him." I lied, it could take a long while especially if the man Klebert lived away from the barracks and didn't drink heavily with his comrades in arms. "Eclair says he will give me some gold Livres coins to get me to Saumur and back. There is no better time and opportunity than now but you must let Eclair think I'm doing it under force. If he thinks I've altered the plan by disclosing and telling you the true details then he may start to think I'd double cross him in other ways."

Caroline after a long while of gazing out to sea eventually spoke.

"Alright, I think it's ludicrous and I have a feeling I'll never see you again."

Caroline once again had her head bowed between her legs seated on the stoney shingle, unable to stand and weeping uncontrollably whilst inhaling deep breaths. What had I done, should I abandon my manhood, my yearning heart, should I spend the rest of my life in a sad state for the sake of my wife and surviving son's happiness? I knew that I should for so many reasons, morally being the most obvious, abandon my dubious and likely to fail intentions. But I had become perversely driven, I knew I was obsessed and I hated myself for the weakness of being unable to control my emotions. However I felt some relief in confronting this first hurdle of informing and telling Caroline of the impending actions, I spent the next two days reassuring her that the quest and plan was sound and I would return triumphant despite knowing in my heart it would be very unlikely.

CHAPTER 20

Anna meets Lucille

The Klebert household was quiet as Lucille woke early as normal, she heard the first morning crow of the cockerel which was followed soon after by the sound of carts and waggons passing by her bedroom window delivering the produce to the market that was at the bottom of the Rue Bouju. She didn't disturb her husband who was sleeping deeply beside her as she knew he'd been away on campaign military business and usually rested for a long period after returning. He'd either satisfied his sexual urges whilst away or with Frances the night before or worse still for Lucille would awaken in an amorous mood and so she was even more determined to make a silent exit from the marital bedroom. She therefore gingerly closed the door behind her, entering the hallway and descended the stairs. Here she would normally see the maid Frances beginning her duties but this morning she was surprisingly absent, Lucille assumed she had slept in but was suddenly aware of voices from the kitchen and service quarters below in the basement. Lucille was not a prude but the house rules must be obeyed and it wasn't permissible or acceptable to receive guests and certainly not without permission and therefore Lucille rushed to investigate, the kitchen door was thrown open where the two ladies in work clothes were chatting.

"Who is this? Why wasn't I told that you were entertaining, you know the rules!"
In truth Lucille was astonished that there was a petite and fair-haired lady with Frances and not a man although her husband Klebert would have certainly been outraged had there been with his possessive nature towards all women which included the kitchen maid.

It was usual for Klebert to find himself in the company of Frances, a small gold coin occasionally given as a guilty extra gratuity for any sexual needs of Klebert which Frances had no power to refuse. Klebert had brought Frances from an area near Marseille in the south and explained her presence to Lucille as a lost and poor girl in need of help; he said she would be a valued servant to the household and passed off her presence as a gift for his wife! Of course Lucille knew the truth and strongly suspected that the same ridiculous story was about to be repeated.

"She arrived last night, your husband told me she was here to work and left her in the kitchen requesting that she share my bed. Apparently it is an arrangement for one night only!" Lucille tutted and went in search of her husband for an answer, with Anna discreetly following; she sensed a heated argument was about to happen and any friction involving Klebert could lead to her learning something to her advantage; any sign of hubris and discomfort for Klebert would also be enjoyable.

Klebert was still asleep when the bedroom door was loudly opened as it slammed against the large wardrobe and Lucille began her questioning.
"Who's that woman you've brought into the house and forced into poor Frances's bedroom? Bloody hell, have you no self control? This one's not even young, she's my age with some middle age wrinkles about the eyes, granted she's beautiful but old by your usual greedy randy standards. Another bloody mouth to feed I suppose and she doesn't look like a hard worker."

Klebert answered angrily.

"Get out, I was sound asleep you imbecile. I'll explain later when you've calmed down." Lucille knew not to continue an argument too long with Klebert as after a few minutes he would become agitated, irate and volatile. Lucille could vent her argument but only within the initial time frame and so she'd learnt to make all relevant points quickly, she left the bedroom in the same haste as she entered it and encountered Anna outside the room.

"What the hell are you doing up here, spying outside my bedroom? You might be of interest to my husband but get back to the kitchen." Anna replied in French, in a confident and perfectly delivered manner.

"I've been kidnapped by your husband, you have no right in making me a prisoner here. If you treat me with respect I'd be grateful."

Lucille was taken aback by the manner of Anna's presence, her deportment, her understanding of her situation. Lucille also felt ashamed of her husband's behaviour who she knew was capable of kidnapping, and had a dreadful loathing of his attitude towards women. There was also a slight sense that perhaps Klebert had met his match with this woman and secretly with her first impressions admired the new house guest.

"We'll speak about this later, what's your name?"

"My name is Anna, I hope we can get on well until I'm able to return to my family in England. I'm sorry I listened outside your bedroom but I must know what your husband intends to do with me. He won't force himself on me without me fiercely rejecting him!" Lucille nodded and in doing so showed that she fully understood the predicament Anna was in. She suggested Anna rejoin Frances with a slight smile of kindness.

Klebert eventually surfaced from his slumber but was in a foul and aggressive mood, he found himself trying to explain Anna's presence in the house.

"She speaks good French, I found her alone and destitute in

England and I thought I was doing her a favour, and you, by bringing her home to help out here. Maybe I shouldn't have bothered if I'd known your attitude would be so hostile. You're bloody ungrateful."

"She's certainly bright, perhaps she'll work out alright." Lucille wasn't prepared to argue any further, she knew it was futile to do so and deep down she wondered perhaps whether there was something enchanting about Anna. Klebert had made his point but was determined to pursue the merits of Anna's presence further.

"She's Irish you know, she hates the stuck up superior and arrogant English more than we do, she and her countrymen were invaded in Ireland by the English and made to do all sorts of awful things."

Klebert was pleased in his belief of persuasion towards Lucille that the argument had been won, that it was settled that Anna would stay and work in the kitchen. He sat back in the salon chair smoking a strong French cigarette and considered his next move of how he could ingratiate himself into Anna's favour, showing her around Saumur and spending time with her wasn't enough, he told himself. Other conquests were persuaded by the local wine, women of a better class which rarely came along needed better quality wine from Bordeaux or the sparkling variety favoured around these parts but something told Klebert that he would require so much more to make love to Anna. A promise of a return to England and reuniting her with her daughters had been made as an initial attempt at seductive persuasion and in a friendly manner. Klebert didn't want to force himself on her, such was his deepening sense of emotions towards her, nor did he wish to blackmail her into reciprocating love and so he became once again melancholy. He spent the morning mournful and then made his way to the main streets of the town where the bars and base entertainment was found for the military personnel of Saumur. He would consider his next moves over some Saumur red wine.

After the front door slammed with Klebert's exit Lucille decided to show Anna around Saumur herself and get to know her more, there was something in her nature that fascinated the lady of the house, something unlike any French maid or indeed French ladies and comrades known to Lucille. The added interest of a foreigner, the Irish accent, the manner she spoke with which was not as subservient in status to Lucille but almost an equal within the household added intrigue and interest. But most of all she believed Anna would stand up to her husband's unpleasant behaviour. Lucille once more wondered whether she'd found an ally, a house companion, perhaps so much more than another domestic servant and sexual distraction for her despicable husband.

Lucille found Anna in the kitchen and asked her to come for a walk, the polite request greatly irritated Frances who whilst knowing her lowly status and position with acceptance and even at times abuse was upset to see herself usurped by a foreign supposed fellow domestic however decent she appeared.
"Will you come for a walk with me Anna, I'll show you Saumur and we need to talk about arrangements and if I can help." Anna affectionately smiled at Frances and respectfully at Lucille as the two ladies set off into the street.

It was the hottest part of the day and Lucille gave Anna a spare parasol from the hallway stand to protect from the sun.
"It gets very hot here and the further south you travel away from the Loire even more so. We tend to rest and sometimes sleep in the afternoons but today I'm happy to walk with you if you don't mind."
"No, I'm happy to be out walking. At home we work through the day, sometimes it's warm but not as hot as this. My daughter Sarah is being schooled by the priest and his helper, she's still young so in the afternoon I do housework with my elder daughter Mary. It's a pleasant part of the day before my drunk

husband arrives home." Anna found herself able and willing to impart, intentionally stated, personal information to make a connection with Lucille; both ladies had apparently wayward husbands and Lucille, filled with some pity, now knew the names of her husband's captive's two daughters.

"Your youngest daughter is schooled by the priest! Is that one of your English priests?" Lucille asked inquisitively. The French had their religious wars and drove out most Huguenot Protesters but still saw the English enemy bound up with the complex issues of their Protestant nature. "I shouldn't tell anyone you're a Protestant, we're Catholic's mostly here. It doesn't bother me though!" Lucille's face showed an indifference to that of any religious denomination and Anna was able to empathise yet again in order to ingratiate herself further.

"I was brought up Protestant but I think your husband believes me to be Catholic. In Belfast I knew many Catholics and their ways, it's not hard for me to adapt to either faith or none whichever way the wind blows! In England my daughters have been schooled in the English church, I teach them politely to respect both schools of thought. They're clever girls".

The ladies reached the Loire, having crossed over the market square at the bottom of the street, and decided rather than make their way towards the busier part of the town, where there were more amenities and attractions, they would stroll in the more shaded direction under the strategically placed Boulevard trees along the river, heading west.

"Do you have children, Lucille?" Anna asked with genuine interest.

"I have a son, Pierre. His father died after the 1789 uprising. Pierre took his father's death really badly and is now a strong supporter of Napoleon so he joined the army. He's garrisoned in the north, he writes to me often and thinks he will be at war in the east soon. I hate the fact I may lose him to more violence and war with Austria or Prussia, I don't care about these countries and the arguments. I don't think the French people care either, we revolted for food and equality not more war. Each regime lets us down!" Lucille became tearful whilst showing concern for her son's safety.

"It must be hard having a son in these times. My husband was in the army but didn't come to harm, I think he was too busy drinking to be able to fight anyway. He deserted from the army after I met him in Ireland, so we live in England where he's not known to the authorities. We're married in name only but not biblically as people understand marriage, I let people think we are as it suits his new identity. He's a weak man." Anna was happy to confide in Lucille, the ladies were comfortable in each other's company and rested after a period of strolling, they leaned against the stone wall that formed the river bank defences, and watched the flowing river pass by.

The sound of the water tumbling over the rocks and boulders that bordered the edges of the Loire provided a peaceful backdrop to their continuing conversation.

"Do you think I have to seriously worry about your husband's advances, he hasn't raped me yet and there was an opportunity in Roscoff ? I'm sorry to ruin the mood but as the night gets closer I have to consider what to do!" Anna took her gaze away from the Loire and by looking straight into Lucille's eyes forced the issue. There was a pause in conversation as Lucille averted Anna's gaze and looked back to the river where some small boats and rowers were heading towards the centre of Saumur, she spoke thoughtfully while looking into the distance.

"He's not like the rapists you would imagine, he's not violent towards women, he's not an aggressive threat. Most men in my experience have a daily desire, a morning and evening lust for gratification which is rarely matched by a woman and Klebert is no exception. When we first met I didn't mind the frequency, and indeed at times welcomed it, but after a while it became a nuisance so I enjoy his time away on service and in truth I don't object to his attention towards Frances, am I complicit in her rape or his pestering of her? Is this the natural course of events that your church and mine expect and teach women? Maybe it's not the church but the natural order of things since we were all descended from savages. How can a man not relieve himself without a woman regardless of permission? I think if you ardently refuse he won't use force!" Lucille appeared so wise to Anna.

"There is such a man at home who I believe wouldn't pester or have expectations and would never become assertive without permission! But you are right, a good man is a rare thing, they are through education and base instinct few and far between. I'll do what's necessary to get home but allowing such an act would be the last weapon in my armoury!" Anna showed stern resolve and Lucille understood very well that Anna couldn't be a consenting house companion to her husband in the same way as Frances.

"Klebert won't return until late tonight, there's an attic room we'll put you in when we return. If Klebert returns from the bar in an amorous mood, he will not attempt anything with you in a room so close to me. He'd be too embarrassed in such close proximity, that's why he feels able to when sneaking down to the basement kitchen room to see Frances."

"Thank you." Anna said in the knowledge that for another night she would be free of unwelcome advances and with each passing day she had the opportunity to learn more to her advantage, to manipulate the situation, to befriend allies with the sole objective of a return to England.

Klebert sat in the window of the bar having reluctantly had conversations with the men he'd been with on the Sussex raids. David was the first but still smarting from the incident on the journey home with Klebert and Anna he didn't stay for long and certainly didn't bring up the topic of whether Klebert had been successful in having sex with Anna. Ordinarily the two men would discuss in detail any bedroom activities. But with regard to the fair Anna the conversation was off limits! Other visitors to the seated window area also realised that Klebert wasn't in the best of moods so he mostly drank alone. His thoughts were of course, of Anna, her beauty, curvaceous but petite frame, her sparkling eyes, fair hair and lightly tanned unblemished skin. However hard he tried to think of other matters, his mind returned to the girl from England. After two bottles of Saumur vin rouge and a liberal glug of Cognac he decided to tell Anna of his feelings once more, he set off into the street for the return home in a determined and excited state.

◆ ◆ ◆

"I think this attic room will do, you can give it a good clean tomorrow. I've put a few of my clothes on the chair and Frances has also donated a few. Klebert will go looking for you in the basement and Frances has kindly said she'll try and distract him tonight down there. If he insists on seeing you tonight and comes past our room then pretend to be asleep, if he becomes threatening then shout out for help and I'll pretend to be outraged. I think after this he'll lose his ardour." Lucille seemed confident that the plan would work.

"Thank you, I'm truly grateful," Anna said.

Sure enough Klebert made his way to the basement in search of Anna and in a raised and semi drunken state asked.

"Where is she, where's Anna?"

"Your wife has been very friendly with her all day and offered her a room to herself in the attic. Why don't you stay here, you'll be happier down here tonight!" Was Frances persuaded by the mistress of the house, Lucille, or did she find something attractive in Anna's nature and kindness and therefore willing to help? Either way she realised the distress Anna would be in and particularly if forced to accept Klebert's company, as she had herself done so many times before, she felt a sense of benevolent virtue, perhaps she would be rewarded in some way, it's good for the soul to do kind things, she told herself. Klebert considered his options and took the easiest one, the maid in the basement who was available without the need for persuasion or seduction would be the best for his relief, sadly tinged with alcohol-fuelled anger. On previous occasions there had been some tenderness from Klebert towards Frances during his nocturnal visits to the basement and yet for the first time there was no warmth, obviously Kleberts mind was elsewhere. Frances was aware that this could be the last visit from the master of the house; his interests would pester elsewhere and because of this Frances had a sense of unease. Her position in domestic service was guaranteed by her availability in accepting Kleberts advances.

Klebert initially became aroused in his amorous act but for the first time ever he hesitated from his raised position above Frances despite her attractiveness, her warmth, affection and seductive womanhood. He lost his biological urge, failing could not be blamed on the excess of wine, it could not be explained by Frances's lack of appeal, she was as beautiful as ever in most men's eyes. Klebert realised that his failed erection was a sign of a problem of the mind and in frustrated shame he fell to the side of Frances where he had decided to sleep the night, he realised that to reach the one who he wanted the company of would mean an argument with Lucille, that this hurdle of the attic bedroom before him would ruin any further action that night and could hamper his cause going forward. It didn't occur to him in the moment that Lucille had intentionally created this obstacle for Anna's protection, had he done so it would have caused extreme anger, this realisation was deferred until the morning! He spoke coldly to Frances with the twin senses of embarrassment in his loss of manhood and a new sense of confused guilt.

"Cover yourself up now Frances, don't embarrass yourself further. I'll sleep here tonight, move over."

The first horse-drawn carriage of the morning made its way over the cobblestones of the Rue Bouju in a slow and hushed manner deliberately so as not to wake the street inhabitants sleeping, only the service quarters in the basement and kitchens would hear the horse's hooves and wheels passing over. Frances had become so accustomed to the sound but Klebert was not and was himself a light sleeper even after a large volume of wine from the previous night's festivities. Klebert gently raised himself from the bed realising his chance to speak with Anna in peace and away from the sleeping ladies, without disturbing Frances who lay beside him he left the room and silently made his way up the three flights of stairs taking particular care to be quiet when passing his own bedroom and entered the attic room where Anna lay.

Klebert gazed upon her face after entering the small dimly lit room and saw Anna peacefully sleeping, her breathing slightly heavier and her mouth with full lips parting periodically with each exhaling of air, an occasional twitch around the right eye furthest from the pillow. He was aware of all the ageing issues that come to a woman of Anna's maturing age and yet, despite her not being in the first flush of youth that would normally attract the lustful nature of base men and Klebert's previous advances towards many younger women, he found himself mesmerised by her beauty. He was unable to wake Anna from her sleep as was planned, frozen in the moment of enormity of his actions, a sense of guilt, heartache and yearning, in physical and mental torment as he stared at Anna's face and body, what hold could this woman have over his behaviour, his judgement, his emotions? He was filled with a heart wrenching pain! This was not a crush! It was developing into an unpleasant and painful love, a powerful love that poisons the soul, that leads to such strong passions that destroys all before it, like a Shakepearian or French romantic tragedy. With a tear in his eye and a sharp intake of breath, purposefully stifled to prevent awakening Anna, Klebert turned and left Anna sleeping. He sank to the floor outside the attic bedroom and forlorn looked to the floor, completely lost in the moment of his frustration, hurt and grief. He had no idea how to put right his impetuous and evil kidnapping or control his emotions.

CHAPTER 21

Eclair confirms the plan

Eclair arrived this time alone, I saw him walking up the lane leading to our farm and therefore there was no need for Caroline to be aware of his visit. Had she known she might through frustration have disturbed us, scuppered the plan, let on to Eclair that she knew it was a staged enforcement of me and my involvement and thereby she may have ruined everything. I ushered Eclair away to our previous meeting place to hear the details.

"The date is set, I'll arrive here with the Coachman next Wednesday around four o'clock in the afternoon and we'll set off to the two destinations where I'm due to drop off, although this time I'll not deliver but collect unbeknown to the owners. Then, along with the allocation here for Mr Watson, I'll meet two brothers named Charles and Edward from Cranbrook. They'll arrive here at eight o'clock and the whole load will be sold and I'll take the gold, and later give you a share after the Coachman is dead."

"What's the Coachman's name?" I asked in fear and trepidation, knowing of my involvement in his murder, the hardest part of the scheme.

"You don't need to know, it will only add to the difficulty and there is no other way, it has to be done. I've got the hard part, my blow with the bottle could be the fatal part of the job, tell yourself that!" Eclair was hardened to the task, he continued. "The Coachman carries about his person a letter as he speaks no English, it reads in English in the event he is caught and questioned...

> "My name is Albert Smith. I am a war veteran having fought the French in
> a battle in the Kingdom of Mysore in 1799. In a series of loud explosions I
> lost all sense of hearing, speech, and senses. Please be aware of my
> difficulty in answering you if you have questions and should the need arise."

The same letter I have here is identical but in French with the name 'Claud Joubert' and the same battle. You'll put it in your coat pocket just in case you may need it on your journey to Saumur and then return to England or not!" Eclair handed over the sealed envelope and I did as he said putting it in my right breast pocket.
"That's the plan, it's simple and can't fail. Once you've helped me row to the awaiting small boat with our gold and coins, the crew will take us back to the French coast near Calais where I've arranged an undisturbed landing. I'm not due to meet smuggling contacts for two days but I have agreed to arrange a carriage so we have a head start to travel south and at Angers on the Atlantic coast where the Loire meets the sea. It's vital that we have the two days for free passage to make our escape. I continue south and you follow the river inland until you reach Saumur which is about a three day walk. I'll be sorry to part company as I'd like to meet your Anna, but maybe it's for the best, perhaps if I met her I'd also fall in love and duel you for her!"

Eclair's attempt at a joke rubbed salt into the wound of my situation, I still hadn't come to terms with the reality of my

decision, despite knowing that I was committed to the action before me my mind and head told me I was doing the wrong thing. Eclair in his usual customary manner made his hasty exit, he shook my hand and said as he departed in a confident way.
"See you Wednesday at four o'clock, be prompt, be determined, be committed to the task in hand and be alert always. If we stay focused then we'll soon find ourselves in France and with gold!"

Wednesday came like any other day, the farm work still needed to be done for the continuation of its future and Caroline and Tom to remain its tenants in the short term and until my return. I imagined myself to be the hero who single handedly had visited France at great personal risk, killed the murderer of my son Robert and brought back a village maid to her daughters. I also believed, in my flawed thinking, that the estranged husband of Anna would lose any self-worth and respect from the community that still remained and that he may be forced to leave and that I would secretly take his place. I would lead a double life, working on the farm with the pretence of being a good husband to Caroline and yet with moments of wild excitement I would spend time with Anna. In her house assisting in heavier duties in the absence of Albert, and in ecstasy where we would be united as one. I forced myself with a violent shaking of the head to focus on the here and now, in the present. In dreaming of a blissful life with Anna it was becoming a distraction from my immediate problems which were to concentrate on the plan and any slight problems that could escalate and destroy any chance of success. Despite the difficulties ahead the deception was vital that Mr Watson believed me to be an innocent party in the theft and Caroline's account would have to be seen and delivered in graphic and painful detail leading to sympathy so as to convince Mr Watson in order that he would allow us, the family, to stay at the farm in my absence. Tom's account, if he were to witness anything, also would need to show no complicity or willingness on my behalf. I blindly told myself the plan would work and my thoughts once again returned to my persistent imaginary fantasy, that of being in Anna's company.

Eclair arrived at four o'clock accompanied by the hooded Coachman, who he addressed in his native French language, as the horse and cart drew to a standstill.
"There's been a change of plan, we are no longer dropping off here but collecting along with the other two farms. We return here later where we sell the whole load to some friends from nearby Cranbrook, our friend here Russell will accompany us as we need the extra help."
"That's not the plan. Why wasn't I told?" The Coachman was clearly displeased.
"It was a late change, it's all agreed and like you I have to obey orders. The orders come from the top man in France so we must do as we are told. We don't have time to argue!"
I was aware of this heated exchange, it was the first time I'd heard the Coachman speak and his tone was confrontational. I immediately began to wonder whether I could hold him face down under the sea water later and cause his death, he seemed larger than I recalled! I once again conjured up the hope that the heavy full Cognac bottle blow would be sufficient to kill him, even in this wish I realised I was a coward. Why was it acceptable for me to absolve myself of guilt in the murder by hoping Eclair's blow would be sufficient?

The Coachman grunted, he wasn't happy but clearly wasn't prepared to argue the point here in England where at any moment he appreciated that there was danger of them being captured. Eclair once again gave out his orders and we both obeyed, with key in hand we made our way to the outbuilding, opened the door and began loading the six Cognac cases. The Coachman took the first case and was carrying it towards the cart when Eclair softly whispered to me.
"Where's your wife, she must witness your presence!"
"She's in the house, if you come inside with me we'll have the

opportunity. Tom's not there, I've sent him on an errand so if you raise your voice and say you've got someone watching Tom and that he'll be harmed if I don't help it will be sufficient. I'll tell Caroline I'll do whatever is asked of me, when he returns she will have her evidence and the account to give to Mr Watson." I wasn't naturally a deceitful person but I was able to convince Eclair of the subterfuge, perhaps it was because Eclair's mother tongue wasn't English but he believed me, I could tell. I also knew Caroline was a sufficient actress to convince Eclair that she was genuinely concerned about our younger son's welfare.

"Very well, let's go now. Continuer a charger le chariot Monsieur!" The Coachman once again grunted but did as he was told and continued his work whilst we walked into the house. As we approached the front door Eclair cleared his throat and prepared himself to speak in a louder than usual and direct tone.
"Caroline, as you know my name is Eclair and I need your husband's help, I've forced him into helping me. We have someone watching your son Tom in Winchelsea and if Russell doesn't help me today and tonight then Tom will meet with a very unpleasant accident, if Russell helps me both your son and Russell will return unharmed, you must wait here and say nothing and they will both be well. Tom will return first. Do you understand?"
Caroline had prepared herself for the speech from Eclair.
"Yes. I understand." Her lips quivered in fright and she looked terrified and amazed. It never ceases to amaze me the talent that Caroline, and many other people I knew and had known throughout my life, have to act in order to gain help, attention, sympathy or gain support when needed. In this instance Caroline, despite not supporting my cause in fleeing to France to avenge the death of our son, gave a masterly performance so much so that a native English speaker would have been fooled. How many times had I been manipulated by Caroline on previous occasions? I wondered. Surely I hadn't! I considered the irony of Caroline's performance, she knew full well that Tom

was well and that she was being fooled by this trick having been forewarned by me, yet she didn't know that I was tricking her by not disclosing that my association with Eclair was in order to search for Anna. Or did she? I found myself ashamed and hoped the blush and reddening of my cheeks wouldn't show. I too had to act with fear and anger towards Eclair in order to play my part in the deception which I did although I believed my acting performance was far less convincing than my wife's. Caroline had her account to inform Mr Watson and so the first stage of the plan was a success.

"Don't forget, Tom is being watched until he returns here. If Russell does as he is told he will return here late tonight, if not he'll be killed and if you raise the alarm even after Tom's return he'll be killed. Are you sure you understand?" Caroline nodded and I attempted to give her a reassuring smile as we left the house, I gazed back at her standing in the kitchen and almost broke down with the enormity and guilt of my actions. Her expression was of sorrow, pity, anger, loss and grief all combined in a face cold and without pallor that wounded deeply my soul and heart, I knew in that moment the great damage that one human being can cause to another. Why did I not change my mind and plans at this moment? This was my last chance to alter my direction and yet still deluded and convinced by Mary's statement and the lasting memory of Anna I pressed on. I looked back and whispered to Caroline in as best a comforting manner as I could muster. "I'll be back!"

The Coachman had loaded the Cognac crates and was in his seat, I jumped on the back of the cart whilst Eclair went back inside the outbuilding and returned with a smile on his face. He knew where the gold Sovereign crowns were hidden and with a wink in my direction he urged the Coachman on to our next destination.
"Notre prochain arret est Broad Oak avec Wittersham." I knew the two villages mentioned and before long we were turning the bend away from my farm, I looked back until my home

disappeared from sight and wondered if I'd ever see it again.

The second stage of the plan went like clockwork with the typical efficiency that was apparent with Eclair's actions and behaviour, he exuded confidence and I wondered whether it was his confident and easy manner that had led me to this criminal madness. At Broad Oak and Wittersham we loaded the Cognac and once again Eclair seemed to know where the gold crowns and coinage was hoarded, and by the look of elation on his face the visits had been very successful and rewarding. The light was fading fast and we were against the clock to find Charles and Edward who we finally met on the Cranbrook road west of Tenterden.

"We don't have long, there's thirty crates of Cognac here, that's the amount we agreed that you'll be taking northwards to London!"

"Yes, that's right." Charles the elder brother spoke whilst giving me a puzzled and awkward expression, had he recognised me? The rural community was a small one, we shared the same doctor, parish priests and vicars did the rounds, as did magistrates and other officials and these two brothers from Cranbrook were very familiar. I told myself that if they were dealing in the smuggling of contraband then they were partners in crime and my willing participation here wouldn't be exposed. More gold coins were passed to Eclair; we retained one lone case of Cognac to be used for bribery and the single bottle for the awful weapon of murder. Due to the weight and volume of the gold, they were all bagged into one strong rope-handled small sack.

Charles spoke once again having stored the Cognac safely on their wagon.

"We're both signing up, taking the King's orders as there's a feeling of war in the air. If we meet each other on the battlefield then we won't be kind and spare you from death," the boy said, smiling at the adventures that were to come. "This hoard will be well hidden until our return, it's our security after the war. Keep your eyes peeled for us if we meet again, our father is the vicar at Cranbrook so we'll be protected by dad's boss from above but you'll have no help from the Lord!" The brothers laughed and with a turning of their wagon returned to the Cranbrook road. I thought it strange and irresponsible, despite my son's murder, that these two brothers who came from a privileged background would be so foolish as to go to war and yet it was I who was foolish. These boys were about to embark on excitable and legitimate actions, I was facing the absolute opposite and so who am I to judge these fine boys!

Before long we were yet again on our way, the Coachman this time knew where to go as he'd made the crossing so many times. Lanterns were lit on the corners of the cart and with the heavy cargo now gone we made good speed and time as we made our way to Romney. Here we left the horse in good care, the cart was abandoned in the marshes and the three of us set off by foot, sometimes wading in water up to our knees as we made our way for the lengthy walk to the outpost of Dungerness.

Dungeness was a desolate and bleak location with a few huts on stilts for protection to the incoming sea; there was a small raised area of a shingled beach where an army outpost hut was used for two Redcoat centuries that covered night-time shifts. Eclair knew them well having passed through often with his illegal loads of contraband, for the price of two full Cognac bottles each, the two drunken army squaddies would turn a blind eye. As we drew nearby and Eclair explained the process and toll that was needed for easy passage it occurred to me how useless they would have been had the murderous raid landed here. The soldiers stationed on the extreme of the marshes were ridiculous; no raid would be made in such a desolate and inhospitable place making the outpost nonsensical. Regardless of the stupidity of the guards' presence they were easily bribed and therefore insignificant as we passed through.

There were a few small rowing boats anchored to posts around the huts and one of which was our means of travel out to sea and our rendezvous with a larger fishing vessel and passage to France. This was the last and seemingly easiest part of the plan, only this time it would involve a murder. I was filled with a sickness, a gut wrenching nausea the likes of which I'd never experienced before at the thought of this necessary but fearful deed. Sure enough the two guards were in residence, standing outside the hut that was lit by lanterns on the veranda and a raised metal-work basket where the evening fire was lit for hot water and the last warmth before the long night duty ahead. Cognac would keep the cold out until a stupor set in over the night, and Eclair greeted the men as great friends.

"Hello there, all quiet as usual?"

"Hello, Frenchie boy. All is quiet, nothing ever happens here until our Cognac arrives." The Redcoat smiled at the prospect of Cognac arriving.

"Here it is as usual, one bottle extra tonight. You two are the best squaddies in the whole Redcoat army, that must be why they put you here on the marshes!" The two soldiers guffawed loudly at the Frenchman's ribbing; they liked Eclair and enjoyed the Cognac even more, especially with the extra bottle which would be argued over or decided with dice by them later. Eclair broke open the case containing the six bottles and passed over the five for keeping a blind eye and allowing passage. They eagerly took the bottles and disappeared into the hut shelter leaving Eclair with the one bottle which customarily was opened once he and the Coachman were under way on their return trip to France.

"Alright, let's go." Eclair gave me a knowing and determined look that said, this is the moment, this is the time, you know the plan! We neared the rowing boat with oars inside and Eclair spoke to the Coachman who was nearest to the craft, "loosen the boat." The Coachman leant forward with his right hand around the post that anchored the mooring and with his left hand untied the rope's knot that was on the water line. "Now," Eclair shouted as he stood behind the bending Coachman. Eclair's right arm was raised over his left shoulder, his right hand tightly gripped around the neck of the full heavy Cognac bottle and with a fast and swift diagonal descent a shocking thudding crack sound came from the impact. "Hold him by the shoulders and push down," ordered Eclair. I rushed forward and stood with one leg either side of the Coachman's body that was face down in the water and moved each of my hands towards his right and left shoulder blades. Despite the darkness and the muddy marshy water, around two feet in depth, I could see a haemorrhaging of blood oozing from a wide wound in the back of the Coachman's head and the body was lifeless. It was an awful and distressing sight but with a sense of relief I knew there would be no need to fully obey the plan and the order to push the dying or dead man beneath the water line.

"It's done, he's dead." I whispered to Eclair so as not to arouse the redcoats on duty, not that they would have left their drinking den, the remote hut! Eclair by now had taken the boat and sat in it with his face looking out to sea, I jumped in eager to put distance between me and the lifeless body that gently floated amongst the marsh reeds. I faced the Kent coast, took hold of the oars and rowed out to sea full of shame and self loathing.

"We did it, well done. The rest of our lives will be easy and wonderful. I can feel the warm sun of Corsica already." Eclair was clearly delighted to be rowing away from England for the last time, but I knew my troubles lay ahead so I gave a wary and slight smile of acknowledgment only and continued to row.

About fifty meters away from the shore line I could see the lantern from the soldiers hut and I thought I could hear, despite the lapping waves around the boat, the sound of laughter from the drinkers inside. To the left of this sight I then saw a chilling and frightening vision that held me frozen and in the fear of the moment I nearly dropped the oar in my left hand. Staggering on the waterfront edge was the standing body of the Coachman, his white face ashen with a gaze that I knew would haunt me for the rest of my life. How could this be? He was dead in front of my eyes! The petrifying enormity of his still being alive struck me, I could never return with this man alive, he would surely look for revenge at the farm and hurt Caroline and Tom, he would visit Mr Watson or criminal associates for assistance in his retribution and in either scenario my family would suffer. In my cowardly stupid act of not making sure that the Coachman was dead I had cut off any chance of my successful return. For a moment I considered letting Eclair know but then I realised this would mean delaying any departure and escape, it would mean an open and violent confrontation with the wounded man and it might force the Redcoats into action. There was no choice left to me, I had to keep rowing, I had to hide the news of the Coachman being alive from Eclair who would be furious, I had to look to a future of either failure and death in an alien country or the possibility of finding Anna and escaping, perhaps to an unknown third country. I knew in my heart that if I found and freed Anna she would insist on an England return to her family, of course she would, what devoted mother wouldn't? My plans, my intentions, my obsessive yearning and my focus were in ruins and lost in despair, all because of an unknown Frenchman living on the English coast!

As I rowed further out to sea I desperately looked over the right shoulder of Eclair and back to the shore. I longed to see the body of the Coachman fall to the sea with a visible splash but the darkness prevented this. I tried to concentrate and yet any clear sight disappeared as I tried to convince myself that I hadn't seen the standing staggering figure, but I had, I desperately tried to imagine that I'd seen the Coachman fall, but I hadn't! This was a nightmarish torment as I once again contemplated the plight of my wife Caroline and Tom, now in the worst kind of danger! I was unable to go back and loathe to row further out to sea but with no other option, in desperate misery and without conversation or eye contact with Eclair I rowed on.

CHAPTER 22

The channel passage and French coast

I looked back to the shore again but it became almost invisible to the naked eye, only the faint glimmer of the lanterns on the soldier's hut remained. My heart was in desperate shock, such a small and insignificant sight in itself to see the staggering Coachman on the shore line and yet such a vision to shock my soul knowing the consequences. I considered the permutations of the Coachman not being dead, he should have been drowned by my hands, such a simple task to put weight against his shoulders and without looking at his face and hold down long enough to make sure! My stupidity had led to this miserable torment, the Coachman, if alive, would have needed help and the drunken soldiers would I assume have assisted. Once aided, the Coachman may disclose his identity as a Frenchman; this was unlikely. Surely he would use his false English identity to avoid capture, pretend to be unable to speak due to battle and then once at large make his way to his criminal friends and allies. Then with a sense of retribution that would lead him to Caroline and the farm, the idea of harm to Caroline, a true innocent in my actions, brought such awful heartache.

My only hope was that the Coachman would die quickly of his

wound and fall once more into the sea, or would be dispatched by the soldiers on duty or would be revealed as a Frenchman with a false identity and shot. But I was clutching at straws, I had to consider the worst case scenario, that my ruse and assistance in the theft would be discovered along with my friend Eclair. I decided to say nothing to Eclair, it was now too late to return regardless and in telling Eclair my Saumur journey would be so much harder without his assistance. I was also too cowardly, would he attack me, would he and his friends on the fishing vessel before us simply throw me, after a punch, into the sea? After a long stretch of rowing we reached the awaiting vessel that would take us to the Normandy French coast.

"Say nothing, remember you are a Frenchman who has lost the power of speech. Only use the letter confirming your new identity in an emergency or if captured. Avoid eye contact with anyone and never show an interest in what's being discussed for fear you'll be invited into conversation. These are innocent fishermen who won't question us, they obey their orders. We'll soon be in France, we'll avoid the criminal contacts I have by bypassing them as we dock further south. Then with all this gold it's south and the Loire before you know it."

"Very well. I won't speak from now on. I am grateful to you Eclair for helping me, I can't tell you how much I appreciate your kindness, you are the only friend I have. I may have made an awful mistake in leaving England but I'm truly grateful for you. God bless your kindness."

Eclair seemed surprised at the outpouring of sentiment and emotion.

"I'm not sure whether God would or will bless me Russell, I may be a lost cause. I'll have time to repent my sins in Corsica over a lifetime of excess, you may be coming along if your Anna can't be found unless it's back to your farm!"

We boarded the fishing vessel and Eclair with a knowing nod acknowledged the head man, two gold coins were passed over and within a short while I was aware that the boat was underway back to France. I was tired from the rowing and dejected from my haunting memory of the Coachman's ashen gaze. I found a small bench attached to the wall and despite my anxiety, I slept deeply.

I woke with a crick in my neck and a severe headache, any thoughts of comfort were sadly lacking as I instantly recalled the events of the previous day and especially the last view of the Kent coast and England where the Coachman had stood. I roused myself and rested my body against the boat's wall so as to not fall from the choppy sea movements, I had enough sense not to gasp out my discomfort in English. Eclair gave me a reassuring glare that I knew meant take care, remember your story, that of a war veteran scarred by the battle and with an unseen injury, an injury of the mind! I gestured that I needed fresh air and perhaps the need to relieve myself over the boat's side. Once on deck it was obvious that the crew were aware of my ailment, they nodded in a sympathetic way and none of them attempted to communicate with me either with language or gestures.

I looked towards the coast, it felt and looked remarkably like the coast I'd just left and yet it filled me with fear and dread, a country of warmongering, lack of any respect towards any regime or order, a country where violence appeared to be the first act before dialogue. I feared for my own safety and for Anna on the land I gazed at this side of the channel, I feared now even more for the wife and son I'd left on the other side. I attempted again to reassure myself that circumstances could change in my favour, Anna spoke French and was resourceful, the Coachman could be dead and of no harm to Caroline and Tom! Who was I fooling with such thoughts? Anna was at the mercy of an unscrupulous murderer named Klebert and my family at home facing the wrath of a desperate man in a foreign country hell bent on revenge for his attempted murder! I was unable to reason properly with the twin scenarios of disaster and success pulsing in either direction in my brain.

The boat docked alongside the quay and we disembarked, as per my instructions I said nothing and made no eye contact, I'd been given the letter which was now a permanent fixture in my inside coat pocket. My presence didn't attract any attention, why would it! I was surrounded by busy, hard working French dock workers, fishermen and porters all served by some women bringing water and food to the masses. I was a shabbily dressed peasant amongst many others and therefore blended into the Calais crowd undetected. Eclair gave me the gold with the order to put it under my coat and with one hand keep a tight grip around the neck of the sack, it was incredibly heavy which was still a surprise to me. I knew how heavy gold was from the occasional coin that passed through my hand but never a large bag full like this, the responsibility that Eclair had entrusted to me of keeping the money safe was reassuring and I appreciated his faith in me. On reflection though it occurred to me that whoever he had gone to meet could have been a threat, a cut throat criminal and therefore I considered in my lonely isolation that he may not return. I had never before felt so alone and became fretful and longed for Eclair's return, his absence felt like an eternity. What would do if Eclair didn't come back? I was alone, spoke no French, knew no one and was in possession of enough gold coins that would start a riot amongst the poor and hungry people, thankfully they had no idea what I had hidden about my person.

I tried to remain as calm as possible, I occasionally adjusted my boots and pretended to act like a local but it was unnatural, I was very self conscious and expected to be approached by rogues, the militia or customs officials which I assumed must exist as they did in the main ports of England. After a while I became aware of a lady smiling at me, her right arm was extended and her hand placed on the wall of the storage warehouse. She was attractive, most ladies I knew or had met were, she stood in a casual manner with her left leg just slightly turned outwards in a manner that suggested she had an open gate and strange walk if she were to be strolling around the streets. It suddenly dawned on me that this lady was perhaps working in entertainment for the returning fishermen, I'd not encountered ladies like this in Winchelsea or even the busier port of Rye. Not since my military service in London and Portsmouth had I encountered ladies who traded their attractive beauty for money and on those occasions I was happy to smile and enter into flirtatious discussions but this was a more uncomfortable and difficult situation. I wondered whether to smile but with a hint of a head shake implying I wasn't interested, I then thought a simple smile could lead to an overture to initiate an introduction, I considered whether a disapproving head shake would be the answer but this may lead to anger from the disgruntled lady and I certainly wasn't judgemental. It occurred to me how serious my predicament was, I was unable even to repel the attentions politely of a simple and poor maiden of Calais plying her seductive trade. Eclair's words came to me, "never make eye contact" and so I looked immediately away from the lady, this small degree of rudeness was alien to my nature and character and I felt wretched for doing so.

Fortunately Eclair came into view along the sea wall and jetty, he stopped about fifty yards away and met two men who clearly had been waiting for his arrival, where he had been before meeting these gentlemen I have no idea and I suspected never will. The three men were of similar appearance, perhaps they were all native Corsecans, they certainly looked like thugs, shifty and in deep, perhaps heated, conversation which in itself stood out amongst the bustling dock workers. Was I wrong to judge the three men in my eyeline chatting as crooks? No, I thought not. Working class peasants do exactly that, they work. Groups of fit men of working age don't loiter in the busy streets, they looked like pimps and the image further caused me stress and fear. I looked out to sea and waited for Eclair to return.

"It's all sorted, we have a carriage and we'll be underway within the hour." Eclair whispered so as not to attract any passing French speaker of his English mutterings imparting good news. "They're happy with their cut and will take me all the way to Marseilles, I can get a ship there, I'm bound for home and we'll drop you at Angers as discussed. All will be well my friend." Eclair was clearly delighted with his plans and presumably trusted implicitly the gentlemen on the quay side and so I was pleased for him but still had an uneasy feeling for us both! My future was anything but "all will be well", poor Anna could be dead already, I had no plan as to a successful return to England regardless of what perils lay ahead. I was also full of worry for my friend Eclair, a man who has put his faith and trust in me, has helped me plan a successful venture to avenge the murder of my son, a chance to rescue a woman I'd fallen in love with and I'd repaid him with a lie and placed him in danger. I was scared to tell him the truth, that the Coachman was probably alive and that he may disclose our treachery and deceit, our attempted murder of him, the selling of Cognac belonging to a criminal syndicate involving Cranbrook thieves, and our absconding with the gold. Things were far from well but I remained silent as we boarded the horse drawn carriage and set off.

"We'll travel by daylight, once dark we will stop overnight for the horses to rest, it's also dangerous and suspicious to travel by night with lanterns. It's good news this carriage is taking me all the way to Marseilles, no stops means less danger, less meeting prying eyes and answering questions. My advice to you is to come with me to Corsica, it's a wonderful country with everything a man needs." Eclair slapped his legs in excitement. My own prospects weren't good but I was pleased for him and as I needed a distraction from my pessimism, anxiety and worries I asked him to tell me about Corsica and his memories of home.

"My family had a farm, I had a wonderful childhood growing up there. We had fine crops of olives, grapes, wheat, and we kept some livestock of sheep, goats and chickens. The British were in charge in my childhood and they were good to us, we traded our produce with them and times were good, then the British started a war with Spain and they had to leave. Unfortunately as they left they weren't as pleasant, one soldier raped my sister and with their departure they stole a great deal from our farm. My father was a broken man and suffered great depression, he hung himself." Eclair's mood had deteriorated so much that I wondered whether to distract him or force a change in conversation. I was saddened to see him recounting bad memories from childhood especially after his chirpy mood previously witnessed. However he was now determined to finish the story and it was interesting to learn the history of how I'd become acquainted with this Corsican young man.

"After the British, came the bloody French, what was left of the farm in produce and the house contents were plundered, this time by the French. With war coming now the French soldiers garrisoned there will leave and so you see why I hate the British and French in equal measure, they destroyed my homeland, ruined my parents, abused my sister. I don't feel bad stealing from either of them, I will steal again, kill if necessary without guilt and as an old man living amongst my kinsmen in Corsica I will live my life in freedom." Eclair was sullen momentarily and looked out of the open window at the Normandy rolling green countryside passing by. All of a sudden he flinched, clicked his fingers sharply and bolted to a seated attention, with the upsetting memories forcibly jolted out of him he returned to the cheerful Eclair I knew.

It helped me to understand Eclair, his story, his reasoning for being a carefree and risk taking thief with an understandable and even justifiable reason to choose a dangerous life of crime. I wondered, had I experienced his childhood would I too be living his life! The soporific motion of the carriage, whilst on occasion jolted over larger rocks and rougher terrain, was mostly smooth and so both Eclair and I, facing each other, slouched in our seats and drifted off to sleep. I suspect Eclair dreamt of his life to come, in blissful harmony with the Corsican climate producing bountiful plenty and possibly in marriage and raising a family. My dreamlike thoughts were as usual, the further I traveled away from the coast and sea my memories and concerns of Caroline, Tom and the farm lightened and were replaced by the vision of Anna. Her angelic face with smooth skin, her bright and blue eyes, her fair hair and petite but curvaceous frame were as sharp in my mind and memory as ever and with each recollection of her came the growing butterflies of love in my stomach, they became more heightened as I travelled nearer and in the hope of finding her. I was still under the spell of Cupid and like a teenager in the excitable infatuation of first love I was driven on by this dangerous unseen power.

CHAPTER 23

Anna's daily chores

The days passed by and Anna, now settled in the attic bedroom, became a familiar part of the household. She distracted herself from the ever present sense of loss and separation from her daughters by making herself busy and in doing so became a valued companion to Lucille and help for Frances. The ease of her kind nature made her popular and there was no sense of jealousy between the two ladies in the house as Anna shared her time with each of them.

Klebert had lost all the sexual urges towards Frances that normally happened a few times a week on the return from the Saumur bars. He had also changed his usual routine of prearranged desire towards his wife Lucille; on the one occasion that it did take place since Anna's arrival at the house, Klebert had made love in a changed manner. He asked permission in advance, was more playful and thoughtful in his approach and movement but lacking in any excitement throughout the act or the intensity at the climax. Lucille at first was offended as she obviously realised that Anna's appearance at the house was the cause of Kleberts changing bedroom habits. Klebert's love making was always selfish but the change must have meant he was thinking of Anna at the time and during the act. Lucille considered whether to show her anger vociferously or if there was an opportunity to be had, could she change Klebert's behaviour to improve her own sexual experience, not necessarily for her enjoyment but a more tolerable experience than before.

A daily routine developed in the household which involved Anna waking and in an act of kindness voluntarily helping Frances with the early breakfast preparation followed by morning cleaning and then the trip to the Loire river for clothes washing. Anna was now so well respected and appreciated as a household guest that domestic chores weren't expected of her and yet she willingly accepted and enjoyed the role of a working guest. Anna, Frances and on occasion accompanied by Lucille would spend the remaining part of the day in conversation with the other ladies in service from the houses that surrounded the river banks of the Loire nearby. In the new France, post the Bastille uprising, there was supposed to be less class distinction but inevitably they became socially separated depending on their status of working service, manual labour or level of profession that the individual undertook. Lucille at first found it somewhat embarrassing to be in the presence of the domestic servants of Saumur but because of Anna's being there and the friendly atmosphere they all enjoyed in relaxed company, the social norms and barriers between servants and their employers had been broken in Anna's presence. How ironic that an Irish foreign lady can bring about a lowering of class barriers in a country that supposedly purported to be the model of social equality, once the aristocrats, elite and privileged had been guillotined. Lucille found herself working, nothing was more natural to her than labouring alongside Anna, there was no resentment from Frances who for the previous two years had been the sole "washerwoman" and domestic skivvy.

Klebert entered the hallway from the door outside to see the three women about to set off to the river, the sun was hot as it often was in the late mornings of the Loire, Klebert was tempted to offer his services when he saw the wicker baskets of washing being held, one each, by the ladies. This however would be so degrading for him, a final loss of power, respect and self worth, how could he kidnap a woman as a trophy, tell his wife she was a native speaking servant and then offer to assist her in the daily chores? And yet seeing Anna laden down with his and the household washing hurt him to the core, the woman he had become infatuated with, lusted and yearned for, developed love for, stood before him with disdain and hatred in her eyes whenever he was in her presence.

"Take care ladies, the sun is hot. I hope you find some shade", Klebert made an attempt to smile and to make eye contact with Anna but he failed as the three ladies passed him in the hall. None of the ladies answered him; his mistake in bringing Anna into the household had united his wife and mistress servant into becoming victims of his unpleasant behaviour, now they were further in unison by the cruelty of the kidnapping of Anna, the woman who was taken from her home and children.

Klebert entered the lounge salon of the house and in a despondent mood poured himself a large Cognac that didn't help his condition, he considered what course of action was open to him. Should he leave the ladies and household and admit his defeat against the women! Should he attempt to ingratiate himself with each of the ladies in order to win the heart of Anna, this would be a hard task! Frances would report all conversations to the other two, now familiar within the household her boundaries and tethering in domestic servitude had been altered. Lucille wouldn't be open to a change in her status as wife and lady of the house, despite her loveless marriage, she would never accept Anna as anything higher than a house guest or perhaps to be seen as a female relative or close friend. Lucille's standing couldn't be seen as a shared role with a foreign lady in the eyes of the Saumur people, eyebrows would be raised and whispers concerning where Klebert's attentions would be each night. Anna clearly wasn't a servant, servants don't socialise with their betters or indeed undertake domestic chores together. Finally if all hurdles could be overcome, Klebert would need to have Anna look upon him with respect, regard, some tenderness and if the passage of time was favourable he could induce a degree of intimacy with her. This final goal was looking very unlikely and he'd decided that forcing her sexually was no longer an option, it wasn't possible he knew to rape a girl that he loved! As Klebert considered this with heart-searching pain he reflected on his comrade David who raped the barmaid in Winchelsea and his own guilt in allowing the crime, to Klebert it all seemed so long ago and how he wished to have never been to England.

There was little option left to Klebert; he poured a second large Cognac and having drained the glass decided to follow the ladies and watch them from afar at their work. He believed that there could be some comfort in simply watching Anna and perhaps imagining that there was no hostility or division between them, with the influence of Cognac he would try and live discreetly in Anna's presence, desperately looking for some form of happiness.

"Where did you wash clothes at home?" Frances asked.
"We have a water pump to the left of our church. The ladies who live in the village meet there in the afternoons but it's not usually hot so we work fast, my daughters Mary and Sarah sometimes help although Sarah is still a bit young, we do the washing for the Manor, the local pub and hotel guest houses. We then meet up in one of the many cellars of the village and dry the washing." Anna was happy talking about her life in England but the ladies were aware of the sadness when her daughters were mentioned. "I'll see them again, they are so clever and educated by me. I taught them well, but at the same time taught them not to disclose their intelligence too much, many men don't like intelligent women. I was privately tutored in Ireland by my

family, we owned a lot of land and industry there but I had to move away." Lucille became very interested.

"Why did you leave your home and Ireland if you don't mind me asking? I've heard that Ireland is a lovely country with people like us in their decent beliefs and attitudes."
Anna grinned.

"Ireland is indeed full of wonderful people, each group living there is different and it works well mostly but there are complications that can't be explained by me or as I've found anyone else!" Anna had no intention despite the friendship that had formed between her and the new friends to tell her life story, her talent was that had she been speaking with Huguenots she would display empathy and affection, the same would apply to Catholics, republicans, royalists, separatists or unionists. Anna was truly a remarkable person.

Once on the water's edge the ladies started to rub soap tablets on the clothing they'd brought. Klebert believed himself to be hidden from view and sat about one hundred yards away further to the right and up the grass bank facing the river. He sat with his legs apart and his arms resting on each knee which enabled him to bow his head only looking up occasionally to glance in the direction of Anna and the other ladies busily working. There was a sound of laughter from the group which added to the stress of Klebert who realised how alienated and disconnected he was from the ladies, he instantly regretted his decision to pursue them and reflected not just on his illogical thought process whilst under the influence of Cognac but also that he felt uncomfortable in secretly watching from afar.

An old lady in another group nearby suddenly took offence at the presence of Anna, she'd heard of her becoming part of the Klebert household from the gossiping that took place during the daily chores at the riverside and, unlike many of the other ladies had a specific dislike of the English and enemies of France. It wasn't surprising, there were many French mothers who had lost sons in the skirmishes that took place around the French borders and colonies where disputes were common particularly between the English and French.

"What are you doing here, English whore?" The old lady, despite being in the company of Lucille who's station was higher and therefore with retaliation cause her personal grief and possible punishment, was full of bitterness and prepared to speak her mind. "My two sons are dead, killed by you English and now you're in my country, my town. Have you no shame? Clear off, whore." It was common knowledge amongst the ladies that the old lady, Madam Cresuet, was justifiably bitter; her husband had died in military service whilst defending the monarchy during the early stages of the uprising. After the overthrow and during the "terror" she was herself nearly guillotined as a traitor to the state. Her two sons were then forced through hunger and poverty to enlist into military service and subsequently died in the Caribbean, a skirmish so minor as to not be worthy of remembrance by either combatant country. Her grudge against humanity and all its ills was well founded!

Anna looked directly into Madam Cresuet's eyes and with a slight smile of acceptance and upturned mouth showed the exact amount of compassion and respect needed to recognize and pacify the old lady. Her learning from the school room came to the fore, her talent for debate, her skill at oratory, her knowledge of Cicero and the classical teaching was obvious and her demeanour and deportment was clear to see, the washerwomen of Saumur were transfixed as Anna rose to her feet.

"My name's Anna, I'm not English. I'm Irish, I've experienced tyranny like you from the English masters, landowners, industrialists and those who wield unfair powers over my people. The true Irish people are the same as you, we were inspired by your uprising and revolt as you released the innocent from your Paris jail. We agreed with your philosophy and beliefs of freedom, equal rights and laws for all, and common fellowship. At one stage we rose up against the corrupt regime in Ireland and almost succeeded..." Anna was interrupted by a lone peasant lady with shabby clothing and missing teeth, a sceptic asking why she wasn't still in Ireland.

"Why are you, an Irish whore, here in France?"

Klebert, who had been watching proceedings, had become alarmed by the attention and hostility towards Anna, he rose to his feet and walked nearer the crowd that had formed, swelled larger by Anna's speech that was now inspiring many with greater excitement and yet Klebert feared for the worst. Klebert stood alert listening rather than continuing his descent once he'd realised there was no danger to Anna, he was however still wary, startled and concerned by the last question, would the truth of Anna's presence in Saumur be exposed? Anna deepened her voice, a strong Irish accent roused the audience still more although they were unaware of its origin, she realised divulging the truth would bring shame and embarrassment to Lucille, the truth that Lucille's husband was a kidnapper and, at best, a philanderer and so in the moment she decided not to tell the truth about Kleberts behaviour towards her.

"I came by an accident of fete, forced by circumstances into a change of direction but I will return to England. I'm no whore despite many men of all countries and creeds thinking of me and many of you in that way. I can tell you that I know many decent English people, they are humble peasants like you with kind natures and good morals, they are different from their rulers and masters, they mean you no harm. I have children like you and I will see them again and I don't need a knight in shining armour to save me or help me return." Anna had become aware of the crowd's reaction to her speech, the warmer and kinder admiration towards her tone with sympathy for her predicament, and some were deeply moved. Anna had also seen in the corner of her eye the forlorn and downcast figure of Klebert, who had in anguish shown himself, and hence she'd added the comment about not needing a man as her saviour. It was a gamble on her part as of course she knew Klebert was her only hope of returning to England, but the comment brought pain and shame to an already emotionally wounded Klebert. He was now completely paralysed by guilt and self loathing, in that instant he realised that far from saving Anna it was he that needed a saviour, and that only Anna could give him peace of mind and any form of absolution that could only come from her forgiveness. The women of Saumur surrounded Anna and with her usual humility she smiled and spoke graciously with many of them including Madam Creuset. Anna's speech particularly moved Frances and in an admiring and almost worship-like way she leant forward and gently praised Anna.

"How wonderful, I didn't realise you were a republican with the same beliefs of equality as us."

"I'm not!" Anna replied with a mischievous wink in her bright blue eyes.

The crowd of washerwomen finally broke up after their daily labours which had been an enjoyable delight on this occasion. Thanks to the oration and moving speech that Anna delivered, the ladies felt a sense of elation, an uplifting presence brought about by this attractive foreigner, a lady that had a strong presence to the Saumur ladies as they reached heights not known in their mundane and laborious lives of servitude.

Klebert sheepishly approached Lucille, Frances and Anna as they were returning to the house; he pretended that by chance he had come across them. On seeing Klebert, the ladies didn't welcome him, they avoided eye contact and didn't initiate conversation forcing Klebert to speak.

"Hello, I was just walking along the banks to see some of my comrades. I'm glad I came across you, I'd like to chat briefly with Anna if possible. Is that alright with you, Lucille. It concerns Anna's future here in Saumur." Obviously Lucille wasn't happy, her acceptance of Anna now within her household she considered had nothing to do with Klebert and everything to do with her respect and forming of friendship bordering on sisterly affection towards the Irish lady who had come amongst them. Klebert asking to speak in private and yet be seen in public with a servant, a wife's close friend or relation, or indeed what many who hadn't yet encountered Anna believed was a foreign whore, was certainly an inappropriate request. Lucille however knew that she was powerless to openly defy her husband and so she gestured to Anna with her acceptance, which Anna agreed to reluctantly whilst knowing it couldn't be avoided. Anna made her way with Klebert to the nearest slope of the grass bank where they sat with appropriate distance.

"I heard you speaking back there Anna, thanks for not saying you were forced here by me. Can I speak freely to you? I must speak to you, I need you to understand." Klebert, despite the Cognac drunk earlier, was quite sober and serious, this was his chance to make a reasonable and last-ditch attempt to put things right with Anna. He was desperate, pleading and emotional as he made his explanatory pitch. "When I saw you Anna, in Winchelsea, I do not know why at that moment I forced you to accompany me onto the boat and why I brought you back to France. But the truth is, on reflection, that there was something in your appearance, something in your face, your gaze, your expression, your beauty that appealed to me, your speaking of my language, but then the accent, and I was unable to resist you. I now know I was wrong to take you from your daughters although when I was driven solely by my lust, my passion and mesmerised by your exceptional individual beauty. I have no excuse for my behaviour, only absolute contrition and I beg your forgiveness. I have a longing for your company, to touch you, to spend all my time with you, to wake in the morning and see your face on the pillow beside me, to lie beside you at night with you being the last thing on my mind and sight and then to enter my dreams until daylight where I would see you once more. I know what you are thinking, I have Lucille, a fine and dutiful wife and you are right, she is truly wonderful in

every way but she isn't you. I've lost my dignity, my pride, my self respect, my reason as I spend my entire waking moments thinking of you. I need you to help me, to forgive me, I'm a broken man. Please believe me, I love you."
Anna looked straight into Klebert's face.

"Take me home, to England, to my daughters." Her comment was cold, direct and to the point, there was no need to plead or show emotions of any type, Klebert was indeed a broken man and with tears in his eyes he was unable to speak further.

CHAPTER 24

Autumn in Saumur

The Klebert household continued to live in a state of change since Anna's arrival, a mixture of occasional sadness but also moments of newly encountered joy. Frances had joined the ladies' influence and judgement against the behaviour of the master who with each passing moment had become more ostracised, isolated and remote from all around him. The social norms that used to exist had now gone completely as the three women treated each other with sincere manners and friendship. Frances still undertook many of the harder house chores but without doing so begrudgingly as she had before, where she once knew her place to be the servant and pestered night mistress of Klebert, she now willingly accepted her workload, and without being asked, undertook the household duties. She treated Lucille as a social equal, more like a distant cousin or a family member and Anna as a newly met sister; the three ladies spent long periods of the day together in conversation. Whenever Klebert witnessed the group, between his bouts of drinking in the Saumur bars or isolation in a rear salon room, he attempted to be well mannered and genial but it was clear that he was in a state of distress. There were many awkward moments of silence when Klebert passed each lady individually or collectively in the hallway corridor or in the communal house areas, Klebert visibly winced in painful shame and embarrassment as any overture he made was met with a single word response, a look of disdain and complete lack of respect.

Klebert knew in his heart and mind that the current state of affairs couldn't continue. He wasn't an overly intelligent man but was experienced in life's emotions especially in those felt by base soldiers, that of lust, desire, sadness, anger, hunger and loss. The newly found emotion of love, that he was now possessed by, was the hardest of all and something he had no experience of. He'd been a seasoned and experienced philanderer before meeting Lucille, who was his first wife, he'd developed feelings for her initially driven by natural urges that confused him and many such men into making the ultimate commitment but it wasn't love. What Klebert now felt towards Anna was different, it was the intense love that if not reciprocated leads to misery and sometimes suicide. Klebert had laughed and dismissed many men as fools and idiots for taking their own lives through failed love, either by their own hand or by dropping their swords in the heat of battle. A soldier who isn't concentrating on the battle before him because of a woman is a fool he would say and yet here he was, a fool he thought condemned by his own words and actions. Klebert also knew that a deranged man jilted and rejected in love was often reportedly guilty of murdering the woman in question and often many innocents around them by consequence. Klebert had also learnt of the equally deranged acts of women hurt in issues of the heart such as the tragedy of the Greek 'Medea' who had killed her children in perverse love, born out of jealousy and rage. Therefore Klebert was aware that a course of urgent action was now needed, he couldn't allow destiny and life's events to run their course without intervention for fear that he was on a perilous path of self destruction! He'd think it over with some more wine by day and Cognac by night and commit himself to making a decision, soon!

The washing trips to the river bank, although daily, were shorter each time as the colder weather took hold in the Loire. It was still warmer than in the very north of France but a sharp cold wind swirled around the river funnelled by the banks on either side, any washing of clothing was therefore done quickly. The ladies of Saumur depending on their wealth and status and particularly the poorest made do with a drying laundry house on the north side and so after the quick washing they took the heavy wet loads by foot across the bridge. The sight of the three ladies of the Klebert household was still met with a smile of surprise by many of the passing folk and pedestrians who knew Lucille by sight, reputation and were casually acquainted. To see the ladies from the same house with differing classes and stations, yet all carrying washing and undertaking menial work together caused some amusement but it was clear that each of them was at ease, content and indifferent to the views of others. Once inside the drying house there were many busy groups at work, each group from houses and accommodation located near to each other and therefore for practical reasons they shared the labour of carrying the bundles back to their streets and mostly terraced houses. The single houses and wealthier homes had their own facilities for drying purposes after using the Loire river for their washing needs.

A central fire pit and brick flu gave the necessary heat for drying and warmth to comfort the ladies. The room had wooden racks that were strategically placed in circular positions around the flames, although not too close to attract a smoke smell that would infuse the drying clothes. The "Klebert ladies" entered the well ventilated room and all the workers looked round with a now familiar welcoming acceptance, often in the anticipation of an uplifting and heartfelt tale from Anna. Over the previous week Anna had been encouraged to speak openly and further by the ladies after they'd experienced and heard of her inspirational thoughts on a woman's role within a male dominated society, of the plight of all innocents that suffered and were subjected to the whims of ruling monarchies and political movements of all persuasions. The fact that so many regimes had come and gone and with each one a depressing lowering of living and social standards gave Anna a captivated audience of disgruntled and despairing women. Anna's conversations and speeches weren't like those of great orators or politicians who inspired the masses to rise up in angry and passionate revolutions, instead they gave comfort and were calming and more subtle in their sensitive delivery. She had the ability to show the right degree of empathy, of understanding from a woman and mothers perspective that moved the simple washerwoman in a moving way they'd not experienced before. This was a rare talent and at times a powerful gift that Anna had and that few individuals are in possession of.

A large elderly domestic servant smiled and greeted the entering party.

"Is there any news Anna of your return to England. Do you think there will be another war preventing your return? I've heard gossip in my house service that war will come soon with the British."

"I haven't heard anything yet about war from the household of Lucille." Anna nodded and smiled towards Lucille as she spoke, answering the questions and towards the elderly lady who had greeted them. "There's always a war somewhere and if it's between France and Britain it won't be unusual or unexpected. Each youthful generation acts in stupidity and consequently the warring madness continues, in time the habits and cultures evolve into something better and the people raise themselves to a better level of humanity. We shouldn't worry for the future, we must simply endure the present discomfort. I'll be returning to England soon, a war won't prevent me from a successful return. I have a sense that there is change coming for me but whilst I'm here it's good to see you all. Tell me how things are with you, if I'm still here at Christmas how do you celebrate? I'd like to help with the cooking, the celebrations and work." The ladies discussed a Loire Christmas, the gatherings and communal activities over the period with the children at the heart of the festivities. Anna had cheered the mood as usual from the prospect of war to the anticipated delights of Christmas and the ladies were soon heard laughing from within the drying house.

CHAPTER 25

The Loire draws nearer

We had spent three days travelling and with each day I'd become closer with Eclair and I now considered him a friend, indeed he was my only friend I starkly reminded myself. We were tied by a common danger, at any moment I knew we could be discovered, my origin of birth and murderous cause of revenge and rescue in France, and Eclair a criminal smuggler who'd absconded with the funds he'd stolen from his treacherous associates. Perhaps the plight we were both in heightened and deepened the friendship I felt for him but it also filled me with fear if the truth became known that my undisclosed knowledge of the Coachman possibly and probably not dead exposed us both to greater peril. How could I feel such respectful friendship towards a man I'd openly lied to? I tried to shrug off any thoughts of guilt and comforted myself by the possibility that any bad news from England could do no harm after Eclair had left England and soon to be away from France. We were now just two days away from Angers where we would part company and our friendship would hopefully end on good terms.

Eclair's mood was still good, he had good reason to believe that England and his crimes were behind him, he longed for the sun of Corsica and the nostalgia and memories of his childhood and past helped with his dreams of the future. He began to whistle and at times break into song in a language I hadn't heard before, maybe a dialect but it didn't sound French or English, perhaps it was an old Corsican folk song. Suddenly he raised the bag of gold coins onto his lap from the adjacent seat.

"Here's your share my English friend, it won't be half but it should be enough to get you out of trouble on your route to Saumur. If you travel well and unseen you may find you have enough for part or all of your return and if the lovely lady Anna speaks French you may find yourself travelling back in style and comfort. I'd really like to meet your Anna, like 'Homer's Helen of Troy'. She must be very special, my friend, but I have a bad feeling about your venture." Eclair passed over some of the French gold Livres and coins in a separate smaller bag that he had secluded in an outer pocket. "Try and travel mostly by half light, morning and evening, hide out of sight when you hear passing carriages as they may stop and offer assistance. On entering Saumur from the east there is the garrison so be careful. Skirt around it, there are many beggars in Saumur so you shouldn't stand out but don't let others assume you are with them or you'll be found out, the beggars are often veteran soldiers and will soon learn and discover your true identity."

The next two days passed quickly, conversation with my friend was free flowing, sometimes philosophical, sometimes deep in life's decisions and their consequences but mostly cheerful. The carriage stopped at night in lay-bys where we enjoyed evening meals with fine wine, a new delight for me as I'd only ever drunk Winchelsea brewed ale prior to this new pleasant distraction. Eventually we drew near to Angers, I looked through the carriage window on my left hand side facing the city that grew larger to the eye. I could see the foreboding sight of the walled castle rising up and the huge two spires of the Cathedral behind the striped stone towers. The realisation that Angers was much larger than I expected gave me a sense of trepidation as I had lived solely in small rural communities, ironically it was the size of Angers where the inhabitants were impersonal to each other that would give me the security of anonymity I required. However it was a daunting prospect to think that very soon I would be amongst the throng and bustle of the city and for the first time completely in the absence of my crutch, my sparky friend Eclair. I'd visited Canterbury on a few occasions and Rochester both in my adjacent home county but on each visit I was very pleased to be leaving and back home to my native Sussex marshes. I took comfort from the fact my visit to Angers would be a quick one, I tapped the outstretched foot of Eclair.

"We're almost at Angers, I can see the castle towers and Cathedral within."

"Good, I'm meeting friends there and we'll sleep in the Hospital St Jean beside the St Maurice Cathedral tonight. Church people don't ask questions so we'll be fine for tonight and then tomorrow we'll part company." I gave a careful and anxious nod and before long the carriage arrived and we were amongst the masses.

I kept Eclair closely in my sights which at times was very difficult, we were swamped by chattering and yelling Angers natives all smelling of French garlic, oily food and body odour, no different from English body odour but multiplied in this throng and densely populated hoards. The odd word I understood but obviously nothing in detail, it was hard to ever imagine I'd be friends with this alien group. They were still European but somehow different I thought, their facial features also looked odd, something I hadn't considered and perhaps wasn't true but in the moment as I looked about they appeared to have wider faces, wider eyes and leathery skin. I suspect it was simply my current unease that was telling me that there were differences of this kind, I reminded myself that after the 1066 invasion at home we were all the same peoples even with the influence of the Spanish blood from those that settled after their Armada failure. However I felt very scared and alone amongst this French crowd like no other I'd ever seen or known.

We jostled our way through the square away from where the carriage had set us down amongst other travellers, where porters argued with each other and haggled with the visitors for the passing trade, eventually the crowds became lighter. The faces became friendlier to one another and the French language I heard was in a quieter and more respectful relaxed manner. The smell also improved as more fresh autumnal air was apparent. We passed through the castle gate house and across the cobbled square and made our way towards the Hospital of St Jean where a kind faced monk greeted us.

"Bonjour les voyageurs, vous êtes les bienvenus ici." The monk wore a habit tied by a rope around the waist and was easily identifiable by the circular bald patch on the crown of his head. I had no idea of what order he came from, I was a member of another branch of Christianity, my local English church, and therefore I was unable to relate to him. Concerning my dealings of late and now in danger of more than one mortal sin for lust, envy, attempted murder and theft I felt humbled and ashamed to be greeted by this kind servant of God. He shook hands with Eclair and then me and as he held my hand Eclair explained my unfortunate history as a suffering wretch and in mental torment from the experience of battle. The monk bowed his head in prayer. Having heard of my predicament he said a prayer, I looked towards Eclair who grinned at the sight of God's servant in prayer for me. I certainly didn't find the experience amusing as Eclair did, probably because I knew that I desperately needed the monk's prayers and help for my soul's salvation and not for the reason Eclair had found as an issue for mirth. Deceiving a monk into a false prayer can be added to the growing list of sins I would face on judgement day!

The kind monk ushered us into the dormitory and gestured with his hand to an area to the right where there was space to roll out bedding or use the straw mattresses provided. There were twenty or so other fellow sleepers, some pilgrims of St James making their way to Santiago de Compostela in Spain, others simply impoverished beggars and other lost souls suffering depression and wandering from various shelters across France. The monk with a cheeky smile put his hand into a pocket of his robe and passed over a bottle that he explained to Eclair was a locally made drink from fermented and distilled oranges.

"Take care, it's strong!" Eclair thanked the monk and we settled down with shared gulps until the bottle was empty, this was the last night's sleep I would know in any form of security.

The monk was right, the Orange flavoured liqueur was strong and so I woke up abruptly with a headache. Eclair was already awake, I saw him in the doorway in conversation with another man who certainly wasn't a monk. I could see the two men were engaged in a heated discussion which gave me a sense of heightened worry, it was always possible that we could be caught at any moment and I'd decided that I was leaving Angers as soon as possible. I rose to my feet, brushed off the floor's dust from the night's sleep and checked my pockets. I was still in possession of the letter and of equal importance the money bag. I saw the distressed and enraged face of Eclair approaching me at pace and I knew from this unseen side of his character that there was a big problem.

"You idiot, I ought to kill you. That bloody Coachman is alive and the news has broken that I'm a thief, a double crosser, a dirty Corsican trickster and it's your bloody fault. I helped you and this is how you repay me. You bastard!"

"I'm sorry. He was lying face down, he was haemorrhaging blood, so much blood, I thought he must be dead. I'm so sorry!" Even now I cowardly didn't tell Eclair the truth that despite the Coachman's lifeless body submerged in water I didn't have the guts to force his body beneath the water for a lengthy period. And worst still, that I'd seen him alive, standing and staring out to sea, still I didn't disclose this to Eclair. I knew I'd put my friend's life in danger through my cowardice. Eclair became more furious.

"How do you expect to kill Klebert, an experienced and driven committed soldier if you can't finish off a wounded man already lying at your feet and unarmed? You should give up now and hurry back to your home like a desperate and frightened rat."

Fortunately for me the monk became aware of Eclair's raised and aggressive tone and although not aroused yet by the English language spoken it was obvious there was tension, Eclair looked around and realised he was in the wrong place to become noisy and physically violent towards me. He also realised he'd lost time to make his escape, the trip to Marseilles and passage to Corsica was now a desperate and urgent cause, he had no time to hear my excuses further or become embroiled and prolonged in English conversation.

"I must go, I've got a ship to find my way home, before I'm caught thanks to you. I needed the two extra days before being found out, now it's lost to me. You're lucky I don't have the time to kill you now myself, but I suspect you'll be dead soon. You won't last long travelling through France, idiots will soon be discovered!" I can't say whether Eclair would have killed me but he was certainly angry enough to do so and with justifiable cause I thought. I watched Eclair turn and rush off and despite his criminal and murderous behaviour I genuinely felt regret and sorrow for his departure, he'd been my security so I would obviously miss his assistance but he'd also become more than an ally in adversity. He was a friend, a confidant in my feelings towards Anna, and if my venture failed I hoped he would be my best chance of life as a possible exile in Corsica assuming an England return wasn't possible, which had now obviously become the case. I realised in deep shock that the Coachman would surely, through his contacts, alert the deceived landowners back home, one of them being Mr Watson. My only chance of returning to Winchelsea was with the Coachman dead, my cloak of deception was the fabrication of my being kidnapped which had now been exposed as a lie and in so doing would condemn Caroline and Tom to dreadful danger.

I hurried out onto the streets of Angers where the daily workers were forming and busying themselves for the day ahead. I quickly got my bearings and saw the Maine river ahead and the Loire valley and river to my right. I knew that by turning right I would be travelling up river in the direction of Saumur for the possibly three day trek and to head north would be towards England. For a brief moment I contemplated an attempt to return home, to save Caroline and Tom, to alert them to the danger and uproot them to a safer life hiding in London but the reality of the situation stopped my taking this option. It would take many days to reach the French coast, use the gold coins and then hope for a safe passage back to England, surely by the time I had returned any harm towards Caroline and Tom would be upon them. I decided to press on with my dangerous endeavour, I quickly walked along the river bank and after an hour I'd successfully passed any suspicious prying eyes, fishermen, children at play and habitable dwellings. My only concern now was the farm and rural workers near and bordering the meandering river, I practiced my facial movements of playing a wounded war veteran, my letter at the ready should the need arise for a pretence of being a French national in distress.

I was completely alone which brought about a desperate need to analyse my predicament, had I missed something mentally that would bring some clarity? I considered returning to the Hospital of St Jean and confessing all to the friendly monk. He may help and bring comfort to my troubled soul but this was dubious and I'd have to confess to being part of a murderous plot towards Klebert, I certainly couldn't do this through utter shame, and so in forced solitude I proceeded with my walk. The main problem I had was of the mind. From my experience of living a distracted life in a dreamlike state I was acutely aware of the damage that solitude and loneliness can cause by an overactive imagination. I would undertake imaginary conversations where one justifies their own, but often wrong position, and become deluded, the conversations that took place in my mind were many and repetitive but never gave comfort. I thought of Caroline, how I missed her now, how I was wrong not to tell her I'd fallen in love with Anna, did she know regardless and was now stricken with the grief of betrayal compounded by the trauma of our murdered son and my abandonment? I thought of my son Tom, to apologise for my actions and stupidity, to advise him not to be ruled by emotions but to follow sound good judgement! I thought of Mr. Watson, to plead with him not to punish my wife and son because of my treachery, to beg him hoping that he would understand the ridiculous behaviour of a man possessed by love! But the conversation and imaginary setting that played out the most was inevitably with Anna, a dreamlike existence in Halcyon delight, and so I was still driven blindly forward. I was in desperate need of English conversation, someone to reason with, someone to advise and impart common sense. But there was no one, and so my mind wandered again in a troubled state, eventually after a few hours of walking I found some shelter, an unused wooden hut missing many panels. I decided to rest for the night, cold, hungry, and worried about my family, Eclair and Anna. Perhaps things would appear better tomorrow I thought, although I was sane enough still to know this was very doubtful!

CHAPTER 26

Caserne Feuquieres Garrison

Lucille and Anna finished their meals in the breakfast room and were talking about plans for the winter, what was required for the household and what events were upcoming for the ladies of Saumur. Frances cheerfully sat on a stool by the window, despite feeling at ease and welcome she was still uncomfortable to take her food with the ladies, probably because she'd served the food and this was her last working daily habit of the former relationship between domestic servant and the new found friendship. There was a knock at the front door and the ladies heard the sound of Klebert in the hallway on route to answer, Lucille quickly shook her head towards Frances who was the door keeper and would in former times have rushed to the sound of a knock, she was the guardian of the house entrance. For some strange reason Klebert was on the scene and the ladies looked knowingly at each other believing that Klebert's prompt response was due to his secretly listening at the keyhole where the ladies sat.

A messenger from the garrison headquarters spoke with Klebert.
"Orders from the Caserne Feuquieres Monsieur." A young man, a fresh recruit passed over an envelope to Klebert who opened

it, with an impolite grunt he dismissed the young man with disdain. Klebert entered the breakfast room where the atmosphere had become decidedly cold and frosty as the ladies anticipated his arrival.

"I've been ordered to the garrison, it could be orders for me to undertake more action. Maybe I'll be sent away and leave you all, make you happy!" Klebert's sarcasm was the only defence mechanism left to him although in this instance, his absence would indeed make the ladies happy! Certainly he wouldn't be missed by them but Anna still knew that her best hope of a return to her daughters was to be aided by a man of some kind and one with authority over sea crossings to England like Klebert. It still filled her with hate and annoyance, the fact that she needed to coerce a man into giving her assistance! Klebert, now without influence or any respect from the ladies, launched a verbal attack on Frances who he thought was the weakest lady in the room.

"Why are you always hanging around? You're a servant and don't belong here, get back downstairs." Frances was accustomed to being a domestic servant; years of being in service had taught her to obey orders without showing displeasure and therefore without making eye contact she rose from her stool in a compliant manner to leave the room but was prevented from doing so by Anna.

"I wish to speak with Frances, she's here for me and as I've been kidnapped here by you then indirectly the fact she's here attending me, in this room, is your fault." Anna's tone was so direct, her ever-present thick accent and the power behind her manner informing Klebert closed any debate. He was further deflated and beaten, the household respect he once had as the provider was utterly smashed, his own self respect lost and now he was unable to give simple orders to the most lowly member of the house, the kitchen servant. Before Anna's presence Klebert considered himself as a leader of men, a master of his house, and deluded himself that he was in sexual demand by Lucille and Frances amongst others on occasion. How could he have lost so much, so soon, now with the added heartache and pain of a yearning love towards the lady who had brought all the stress and hurtful turmoil that had turned his life upside down. With his humiliation complete he knew that Anna would never look towards him with affection, he left the room and after collecting his sword and military regalia made his way to the garrison.

"He's a weak man, it won't be too long until I can get him to return me to England. However I think I need to improve my knowledge of French just in case I'm here for a longer period, can I read some of the books in this room Lucille?" Anna asked whilst looking around at the dusty bookshelves on the two inner walls, she knew full well that permission would be granted with a warm smile. "Perhaps occasionally when you are out with the washing please when I won't be distracted by your good company."

"You are welcome, they haven't been read in a long time. I think the bookcases and books were here when we moved in, left behind by the old man who died here." Lucille agreed that a deeper understanding of the French language and cultural knowledge might prove beneficial in the future.

Klebert tried hard to shake himself out of his persistent misery and somber mood that he had displayed to all those around him of late; he knew that melancholy wasn't the right word for his malaise which was a far more serious depression. On arrival at the garrison, a huge Chateau that housed the hierarchy of Officers, Klebert walked through the gates and into the cobbled courtyard where he saw the many familiar faces of his group, comrades in arms, and fellow soldiers. Although he had seniority over those gathered, it was a very informal group without respect or order, hence their ability to be unscrupulous and ill disciplined in battle and raids. No one stood to attention on seeing Klebert but the majority looked round with a nod of recognition to see their leader and friend but some were intrigued to see whether the rumours were true, mostly spread by David, that Klebert had become morose, love-stricken and obsessed with his 'English' whore! Klebert was aware of an awkward silence as he approached the first group of men in the middle of the courtyard, whilst the other groups around the inner Chateau walls also stopped their conversations and began to walk towards the centre so as to hear better the truth.

"Bonjour. What's the news, are we going somewhere soon?" Klebert knew from the peculiar atmosphere of the group that they were interested in gossip and his affairs but he was determined to stick to the issue of the military activities and plans.

"No news yet, the officer said he'll be out soon." The answer came from a seasoned and experienced older campaigner who had the unofficial rank of sergeant, everyone accepted his orders as he was well liked and respected.

"Good, we better muster then", said Klebert, the thirty shabbily dressed soldiers formed into two rows in the courtyard facing the inner gate of the Chateau entrance where the administration officer would appear. After a short period the smartly dressed French army officer appeared and gave a quick update.

"I don't know the political situation, comrades but I have been told that there is tension between us and Prussia and that the annoying and meddling British are always flexing their feeble muscles. Our great leader Bonaparte will deal with them in good time and we must trust in him. Congratulations, the last raid was a great success, not that lucrative sadly but it was good in undermining the English morale, they'll not sleep well knowing we can attack at any moment. There's another raid planned for the end of November so you will muster again in Roscoff in the usual billets you have between now and the departure date and then receive a detailed plan before embarking. Any questions?" There were no questions and the officer turned abruptly and retreated back into the Chateau. He had little respect for the military unit as he knew them to be from the criminal classes in Saumur and in his view they were of little worth unless away on military campaigns.

The men assembled started discussing arrangements for the return to Roscoff; the order for another raid would bring further opportunities for theft, to replenish funds for their needs of alcohol and prostitutes. Some, like Klebert, had households to upkeep, small dwellings with wives that required money to prevent them doing work in the service industry or being affectionate to their landlords. The news of a further raid had encouraged the mood amongst the men and it was decided to assemble in the bar to the right of the Chateau to prolong the enjoyment of their news with wine and Cognac. It would be a long and exciting evening for the militia group of drinkers, with the good news of further adventure to come the celebrations could last for a few days before they each made their way to Roscoff once more.

CHAPTER 27

Russell reaches Saumur

I awoke from the hut with a frozen chill deep in my bones, an uncontrollable shivering and in need of water and food, preferably hot. After some strange, on the spot, exercises in an attempt to get warm I set off again in the direction of Saumur that I hoped I would reach on the following morning if I made good progress and with an exceptionally long walk today. Fortunately I found a clean water trough, in an adjacent field for cows, which was fed by a natural stream so I was able to quench my desperate thirst, my next immediate need was for food as my last meal was from the kindness given by the Hospital monk and therefore I was now suffering from desperate hunger. I certainly couldn't walk for a whole long day without some form of nourishment and therefore my only option was to approach a farm that came into view after an hour's walk and so I practiced my wounded veteran mannerisms and checked my pocket where the letter of explanation would be needed. I steeled myself bravely whilst walking towards the farmhouse door.

My newly acquired criminal mind considered the options available, either I could force entry and with violence, or the threat of it, steal some food. My other two options were to beg for it or I could simply pay with one of the few gold coins I carried with me that were graciously given by Eclair, a generous act I suspect he now regretted. But to hand over a gold coin or any coin of lesser value from my small bag whilst being dressed as a tramp, who'd clearly slept the previous night without warmth or proper shelter, would surely arouse suspicion with them believing the coins to be stolen. The preferred option therefore to beg for food would require some skill on my part, I'd never begged for anything in my life but to do so by playing the role of a veteran soldier with a disturbed mind from battle would take a great deal of wit and cunning. I realised that if I was to succeed and survive amongst the people of Saumur I would need some experience of playing the veteran part and what better opportunity than to experiment in front of a peasant farmer and his family. I hoped that I might encounter a farmer's wife or daughter alone in the house, giving me a more relaxed atmosphere without the threat of an aggressive altercation with male occupants.

The farmhouse was about a hundred meters up a newly ploughed field that faced the river and although different in style and architecture it still was similar to any other farm and gave me a sense of homesickness. I could see smoke rising from the right side of the house and the chimney on that side, instinctively I believed this to be the kitchen and was aware of an open door and the faint sound of conversation from within. I steeled myself once more to the prospect that this could be my first encounter with danger, with capture that could possibly lead to torture followed by discovery and then death. With a sharp intake of breath I approached and entered the kitchen with a polite knock on the door. Despite my walking this far since my sleeping I was still shivering from the cold of the previous night's exposure but now coupled with fear I was able convincingly to act out and portray my deceptive newly adopted character.

"Bon… Jour", I whimpered with a stammer and trembling upper body. I exaggerated the jerking movement of my limbs and hoped it would appear involuntary. This would be my last attempt at speech as advised by Eclair, I produced the now opened envelope and letter from my pocket and handed it to the, I presumed, farmer who was sadly in attendance along with his wife and a younger girl I believed to be his daughter. The three family members sat around the table with the remains of their breakfast, a bread basket with four baguettes, coffee bowls half filled and jam preserves. There were also five freshly caught Trout fish which presumably had come from the river and were perhaps intended for their lunch. The farmer read the note and surprisingly to me didn't seem surprised by its content, perhaps there were many such veterans of war and conflict that passed by roaming the countryside in need. There had certainly been a great deal of violence and conflict over the recent years. I gestured with my shaky hand by holding it up to my open mouth and after a brief period he spoke to his wife who obeyed his command whilst his daughter looked inquisitively at me.

"Cet homme est un soldat touché par la guerre. Donned-lui à manger."

To my great surprise a baguette was handed to me and a full bowl of tepid coffee. I nodded with appreciation and drank the coffee straight down and smiled again nodding with thanks and turned to leave. As I did, the daughter rose to her feet and came towards me with a greeting at the door where she picked up one of the fish and smiled sympathetically as she passed it to me. This small act of amazing kindness filled me with shame and embarrassment especially as I could see that the farmer and his wife weren't comfortable with the extra gift of a fish from their lunch but too polite to counter their daughter's act. I felt wretched, I'd conned and deceived this moral and fine family into giving away food and despite the desperate need and hunger I had I realised how low I'd sunk in common decency to my fellow man. With a pitiful but grateful smile towards the daughter and a tear in my eye I left the farm, ashamed to look back, instead my gaze lowered to the fish and baguette.

It occurred to me, as I left the farm, that had I suffered the trauma in childhood that Eclair had I may have been content in deceiving the kind farming family and yet I had no hard luck story to tell, no disturbed childhood, no heart wrenching excuse other than a desire to locate a woman who I'd become infatuated with. I obviously wanted to kill Klebert in revenge for Robert's murder but this was no excuse to deceive other innocents as I had just done, nor indeed to my wife Caroline at home who'd been dealt the biggest deception of all. I passed through a gate and rejoined the pathway heading up river and as I did I paused momentarily in contemplation and then placed two gold Livre coins on the gatepost knowing that the farming family would be the only ones to pass by this spot and that the money would surely be found by them. It was a large payment in monetary terms but a pitiful gesture of thanks and atonement and didn't lighten my sense of guilt.

I kept the Loire river on my left hand side and followed the footpath where possible, travelling inland where it was needed but importantly keeping out of sight from other travellers. After the day's lengthy walk I became aware of more passing trade and assumed that Saumur might be drawing nearer and so I decided to rest, tomorrow would see me arrive. I found an isolated spot with a good view of anyone approaching and decided to risk lighting a fire in order to gut, remove the head of the fish, and cook it. By good fortune I was successful, the fish and bread tasted wonderful which only intensified the shame that I still felt. With the sensation of an almost full stomach and my labour of the day's walk evading all passers by I felt tired and fell asleep hoping that tomorrow could by chance and good fortune bring me better fortune.

My mood had not drastically improved on waking the following morning, I knew this would be the day that I'd reach Saumur, there would be water fountains, kitchens, cafes and bars but I was under no illusions as to my danger and precarious state. Begging might be easier, to get food from bars, groups and businesses would decrease the guilt I had felt taking from those who may be in need themselves or individuals. There may also be the opportunity to pay for provisions and accommodation with the occasional gold coin but I'd need to keep the pretence of my new character for fear of my lack of French language speaking revealing my identity. Perhaps I could play the part of a drunkard by entering an establishment and yelling "chambre", would this lead to an invitation to a room having tossed a gold Livre or two in the boardinghouse keeper's direction? Sure enough, as Eclair had said, the garrison Chateau of Saumur appeared as I neared the town, another Chateau and church spire lay in the distance and I could see two bridges that spanned the river, the immediate one was the busier with horses, carts and wagons passing between the north and south sides. It was all as Eclair had forewarned me and I took particular care to quickly skirt the outside wall of the army garrison Château.

I knew that to find Anna, if she were still alive and not cruelly dispatched and thrown from the Aquilon, I would first need to seek out Klebert and more importantly not kill him. I would need to follow him to either his household or a separate dwelling house where he might keep a mistress secretly from his family. Perhaps poor Anna may have been put to work in some form of domestic service, a factory or even worse a brothel, my imagination was still fast at work of mostly unpleasant scenarios that could have befallen poor Anna. I quickly steadied myself to the matter in hand which was to find food, water and then this odious and foul dark skinned man, Klebert.

I made my way to the centre of Saumur where I assumed the market stalls and folk would be selling their wares and trading, where amongst the hectic business and bustle I would be less likely to stand out and raise suspicion. I kept repeating the instructions from Eclair, in order to prevent inquisitive conversations I needed to blend into my surroundings and this meant mingling with the other tramps and down and outs. The best possibility of meeting other beggars was amongst the masses, I believed and hoped that maybe one more beggar wouldn't be noticed! Sure enough there was some late morning trade in progress and the bars that surrounded the market square were getting ready for the luncheon trade. A strong aroma filled the areas outside each bar with olive oil, fresh bread and the morning catch from the Loire and after drinking cold water from the gushing fountain adjacent to the church I sat on the cobbled floor taking in the vista of activity. With the warm autumn sun at its height and despite the Saumur locals in full and loud conversation around me I became drowsy from the morning trek that had brought me here in good time.

Although I was hungry, with a rumbling tummy, I drifted off into a light doze until waking abruptly from a severe sharp pain of a boot kicked against my left ankle on the bone. With an exhale and cry of pain I swore, and in the terrible moment of pain my swearing was for understandable reasons in English!
"Drat, bloody bollocks, shit". I checked myself quickly, coming to my senses and seeing my surroundings. A large French man with a holstered sword stood before me still yelling angrily. I assumed that it was merely my presence that was causing him offence and annoyance, had I given away my identity in my swearing outburst? Upon rising in a petrified state I would either need to hit this bloody Frenchman and run or simply, but as calmly as possible, walk away in disgruntled pain. I held up my hand in an act of unfelt apology although not really knowing what my crime had been.
"Pardon monsieur", I grunted and walked away. As I turned a further sharp pain of a well aimed boot hit me in the backside and once again I winced in pain. This time it took serious self control not to turn round, take the knife from my inner pocket and thrust it towards his fat ugly head or heart but my situation was enough to prevent any more stupidity on my behalf which

would lead to my capture and I walked gingerly off still winded and in angry pain. I had a good view of this man in the afternoon sunlight and I vowed to myself that if the opportunity arose I'd knife the bloody French bastard in the back such was my fury in the moment of exasperation. Maybe this rage would die down or reduce but in the moment it was the strongest sense of anger I'd felt in a long time, even the murderer and kidnapper Klebert hadn't instilled this degree of rage. I left the market square and settled in a neighbouring street taking deep breaths to ease my pain and quiet my temper.

By good fortune, and another twist of fate, the attack on me had been witnessed by two ladies passing by with their baskets of dried clothing and fresh bread from their daily work. I'm not sure whether they'd followed me to the neighbouring street or they'd simply been walking in the direction I'd come, they stopped and spoke to me. This time I'd have no option other than to play the part of the war veteran which saddened me as they appeared to be such friendly and kind souls, the first I had encountered since arriving in Saumur. They gave me warm smiles, a form of comfort in my present predicament of pain. Had they been sent from heaven, were they themselves under the influence of a benevolent giving power? "Bonjour monsieur, Pouvons-nous vous aider?"
I instinctively knew that the kind ladies were offering me assistance, I knew they couldn't ease the pain I was in from the attack that they had seen so I shook my head gesturing with thanks and relieved in the knowledge that my true identity yet again wouldn't be detected. The ladies, both in their middle age, were obviously close friends, they spoke for a brief period to each other and then one of them passed to me a piece of bread that was broken away from a larger loaf. Then to my surprise, the lady who appeared to be more senior in her deportment and station in life gave me a clean dry shirt from the washing pile. It occurred to me that unless she was the mistress of the household she may be chastised for giving away a man's smart

shirt, her kindness was overwhelming. So much kindness had been given to me since my arrival in France I reflected, the Monk with his Orange liqueur, food and bed for the night, the farmer's daughter with the extra trout and now two angels with bread and a man's clean shirt. Such kindness almost brought me to tears in the light of my shameful behaviour, my thoughts turned to Caroline and Tom who I knew would be as welcoming and kind to those passing through our home farm in Winchelsea. How I longed in this moment to be out of pain, to be warm in my own home and in this moment desperate for the knowledge of my family living in safety and at peace.

I looked at the angel's face. "Merci Madame", I muttered silently so as not to say my gratitude in an accent so clearly English. The ladies smiled and walked away up the cobbled street where I assumed they lived. I had been on the receiving end of extraordinary kindness to a stranger, the ladies clearly saw me as a tramp or down and out beggar, this impression of vagrancy was becoming so successful I wondered whether I'd ever need the gold coins that I carried about my person. I now realised that to offer the money in exchange for provisions and shelter would surely lead to my being found out, it would be impossible to avoid the slightest conversation whilst passing gold or the lesser coins to tradesmen and looking like a vagrant. Any respectable person would assume they were stolen ill-gotten gains and indeed they were! As the afternoon drew to an end I finished the bread and found a secluded spot to freshen up with Loire water, I dressed in the new shirt which was clearly fitted for a taller man and yet a surprisingly comfortable fit. Whilst dressing I wondered what manner of man owned the shirt, was he a generous man kind and understanding of his washer servant's kindness in giving away his clothing? Was he a professional man or perhaps a priest, would he reflect on the Biblical parable of the offering of the 'shirt from one's back'? I put the man's identity to the back of my mind and finished dressing and in doing so I looked down at the shirt cuffs before putting my coat back on, a large red K laundry mark was embroidered on the right shirt cuff. I once again thought how lucky this man K must be to be in the company of such kind and friendly ladies and that surely his household was a happy place to live! Although successful so far in this manner of living as a beggar I appreciated that it couldn't continue for long and therefore I rested until nightfall before setting off to the Inns and bars of Saumur in search of a man called Klebert and his friend named David. Two needles in a proverbial haystack!

CHAPTER 28

The Saumur hostelries and the encounter with David and Klebert.

The crew of ill disciplined and lowly soldiers discussed their hopes in the next raid, the riches and wealth they might find, the loot that might give them some security, but most importantly some good living on their return. There was also the prospect of the English women they would encounter and what depraved sexual actions that they hoped might follow with or without introduction. With each tempting prospect they discussed future gains another draining of glasses and goblets accompanied the conversation so the soldiers became more and more drunk and excitable. Only one member of the group was visibly seen not enjoying himself to the same extent as the others, the seasoned veteran Klebert, and whilst he consumed the same volume of alcohol he had become more isolated from the group and played a lesser role in the audible debauchery. David was the ringleader, fuelled by alcohol, amongst the rabble and had an extra edge of aggressive exuberance in his drunken manner.

"Those bastards have got my brother Maurice, he might be still held in jail there. They'll pay for that, we should find him! But if we can't, I'm going to kill as many as I can, bloody English."

"He'll be long gone, they won't keep him prisoner. You need to

accept it, I agree though, we'll get revenge on them", said a senior member of the group wrapping his arm in comfort and unity around David. The two men were filled with rage by the alcohol which had intensified their anger towards the English enemy. "What say you Klebert, do you think Maurice is still alive?"
Klebert was on the adjacent table nursing a bottle of Cognac and clearly in a sullen mood, his mind was on Anna and whilst he felt some resentment towards the English for their historical meddling in the French politics and affairs he didn't dislike them with the same venom. Had Anna been of English decent Klebert's feelings may have been more conflicted, perhaps even defensive, but he was able to see and appreciate her as an Irish girl and by her own account historically an enemy of the English. He was however primarily a soldier of fortune who obeyed orders without question and killed whether they be foreign or fellow French citizens.

"He's probably dead, if we'd caught a raider here we'd have killed him instantly so I suspect they have done the same. Maurice knew the risks!"

"Sounds like you are defending them." David was still upset, wild with anger and growing more irritated at Klebert's indifferent attitude and disconnected approach to the group since the arrival of the 'English whore' who had caused Klebert's depression. "It's that bloody English whore who has changed your mood!" Klebert stared at David with an angry flicker in his eye that immediately made David look away and consider whether to take flight. Klebert wasn't prepared to leave his half drunk bottle of Cognac, and in what appeared to be a defeatist stance decided not escalate the argument further, at least not yet! The mood temporarily lightened as the fine Saumur red wine was consumed further accompanied by more Cognac.

❖ ❖ ❖

With my clean shirt and bread in my stomach I went from bar to bar with a small degree of new strength and vigor peering through the windows and doorways looking for men of fighting and military age in the hope I might luckily find Klebert. As it was a garrison town I worried that I would never find the soldier in question and after an hour of walking the streets I rested outside a particularly raucous bar where young and old men were inside and sprawled out onto the cobbles with their drinks. I felt very vulnerable especially having been beaten earlier by a man for no good reason but I knew I must keep near to the noisy heart of the community. I took the role once again of the beggar after quenching my thirst at the "centre ville" fountain and slumped down with my legs crossed occasionally looking around and listening out for a sign. I was very despondent and gloomy as I rested my back against the hard and ridged brickwork listening to the laughter from the busiest bar of Saumur to my right hand side. I'm not sure how long I'd been sitting in this position but the light was fading fast, had I been asleep I wondered as the time passed? I must move soon I thought as my legs began to stiffen and seize up and as I rose to my feet I was aware of an angry altercation from the bar doorway.

"Where are you sloping off to? To that bloody whore I suppose." A shabby and drunken man shouted in pursuit of a better dressed and dark featured man who I thought looked like a Spaniard, dusky and of Moorish descent, he turned around and with his hand gestured in a kindly manner.

"David, I wish to speak with you my friend. Please walk with me to my house. Come and have a Cognac with me and we'll toast our success on the next raid." Klebert's voice was quiet, measured and kind and David was desperately eager to renew his friendship with his lost ally and comrade who had appeared distant of late. David was clearly pleased to follow and smiled as he did so.

Did I hear correctly, this man called out to "David" and it occurred to me even in the evening light that the request from the caller fitted the description of the murderer Klebert. I couldn't believe this could be my chance, could I be so lucky? I'd only heard the name "David" but I was encouraged, with some hope at last. I staggered to my feet and watched the two men wander with their drunken walk towards the alleyway that led uphill to nearby residential streets and a cobblestone hill of terrace townhouses. I followed at a distance far enough away so as to avoid detection but near enough to listen if voices were raised and to observe. Once more I heard the name "David" spoken louder, if only I could be sure of the identity of the other man, I desperately wanted to hear a reply saying "Klebert!" The Spaniard put his arm around the shoulder of the other and spoke softly and affectionately, if only I could understand the content!

"David, I've noticed of late that you've become very annoyed with my distracted mood and state and I'd like to apologise to you. This is how I shall apologise."

I was about twenty meters away and I saw the taller man plunge his fist into the guts of the other man who'd been yelling excitedly and angrily earlier at the bar entrance. The man slumped to the ground and exhaled a loud gasp of pain, I looked around me in case the sounds would bring attention from passers by but the bustling bar was now well behind us, there was no one around so my capture wasn't threatened. The man, now kneeling, lurched to his feet and I saw a flash of light reflected from a street candle beyond the alleyway exit, it was a blade and with a squirting of blood the Spaniard was sent back against the brick wall opposite. I realised this was a serious fight and one that could lead to death, I couldn't be implicated or found nearby and immediately considered leaving but this was still my best chance of finding Anna. My brain and thoughts were held in enthusiastic fervour as I thought of my options, fleetingly I thought if it was Klebert and he was killed how would I find Anna? The Spaniard, clearly wounded from a gash to his upper stomach, drew his sword and with a strike that initially hit the brickwork, descended and almost severed the right arm of the drunken man still in agony from the blow to his stomach. The sword attack saw the man "David" sprawl to the floor and an instinct told me he wouldn't rise again. The Spaniard had clearly won the duel or fight but he looked to be a man possessed by an evil demon perhaps born out of a desperate state of hurt. I wondered what would make my fellow man so incensed as his attack continued. Four or five times the Spaniard, despite his injury, kicked the man now groaning in pain on the cobbles with blood running down on the ground towards me. The Spaniard staggered off up the hill clearly wounded and in pain.

I approached the recumbent man who was gasping for breath, I believed him to be dying and lifted his head slightly from the ground. Despite having no understanding of the French language I knew one or two words that could help me now and so I asked.

"Est vous David? Oui?" The Frenchman nodded, he attempted to speak and as he did I was aware of blood in his mouth. I questioned further, "etait-ce Klebert? Oui?"

Again David nodded. "Est vous frere Maurice? Oui? Once more the Frenchman nodded. As he lay dying I said to him in clear English first and then French. "He's dead in England. En Angleterre il est mort." I could see the man in front of me, despite being in the last throes of his life, visibly shaken and a beastly satisfaction took hold of me as I thought of Emma and my son Robert's attempt to protect her from this man. I threw his raised head from my hands to the floor and as he dropped a final gasp came from his mouth accompanied by a blood trail that splashed the wall behind. My venture to France had not been in vain, one of the prime movers in my son's death and the rapist was now gone. I hurriedly left the scene in search of the man I now knew to be Klebert!

I'd lost time whilst dealing with David but as I saw Klebert stumble away swaying from side to side in pain I was therefore hopeful of catching up with him. I followed in his direction aided by a few signs and spots of blood on the cobbles where he'd stopped to get his breath. I was full of excitement at my good fortune and the prospect of killing this man and finding Anna but I realised that if I were to run after him I might arouse suspicion. I might even be seen and accused of the murder of David and therefore I walked with great speed but not breaking into a trot. My breathing was loud and laboured as I hurriedly rushed up the street in pursuit of the wounded soldier.

My good fortune continued as in the distance of about fifty yards I saw him, wounded and helpless, bent half over and clutching his torso. I was unable to rationally consider my actions and instinctively called out, "Klebert!" The distressed voice in the half light of evening darkness replied.

"Aide moi, sil vous plait." He looked in my direction perhaps thinking I was a comrade in arms or maybe a witness to his fight with David. Was his cry for help aimed specifically towards me, had he seen my features, would he recognise me again, had he detected my English accent, had I become a new threat to him? Many questions came to me.

I rushed quickly towards him, I drew my knife from the pocket of my heavy coat knowing this was my moment, the chance I was looking for, the opportunity to find Anna and finally to slit the throat of the evil man before me. I suddenly realised and believed that to kill him without disclosing my identity wasn't enough, he'd need to know that I was the father of Robert, a friend of Emma's, and most importantly the man that was here to save Anna who'd been savagely taken away from me and her family. With my wicked rage and intent on retribution I drew near the almost collapsed and lying body, how easy it would be now with Klebert in such pain to finish him off. However I was still conscious of the fact I needed to find Anna, he would have to be forced to disclose her location before my blade would be used to kill. I was also starkly aware that since beginning my foolish crusade I hadn't killed, not the Coachman, nor David and there was no certainty that once encountering Klebert I'd have the guts to kill him in cold blood either but I was resolved to the cause and determined. A fair duel would certainly not be a good idea against this swordsman so this was my good fortune, my moment of victory. I was no fool and therefore I would never challenge a man who clearly had the strength and experience of battle to beat me but he was now in front of me, a wounded animal and once he'd told me Anna's whereabouts and had realised my purpose I would enjoy seeing his end.

Fuelled by anger, courage and opportunity I approached and met the full gaze of Klebert, he knew in that moment I was not nearing him to give aid but with a brutal intent. With my raised right hand holding the blade I was about to strike and deliver some dreadful pain but the door, where Klebert stood doubled up in agony, opened and Klebert cried out.
"Lucille. Aider!"
I staggered back and turned, thwarted at the moment of my victorious attack and retreated into the darkness behind me away from the light that was cast from the open doorway. Still worse was the fact that I recognised the lady who'd come to the door and aided Klebert as the same lady who'd given me the clean shirt and bread that morning. What dreadful luck to ruin my chances, to add further complications to my cause, to deny me the justice that I so rightly deserved. How could this have happened, I questioned as I found shelter once again in the darkness of a deserted quiet street.

I must think and reassess my options calmly, would it matter that Klebert was married, a relative or friend of this lady who I now knew as Lucille? Would it matter that I could bring her despair and grief if I was successful in killing this man? If I walked away would I feel wretched and a coward for not satisfying my need for revenge? Most of all, what about Anna and her welfare? I knew in my, now troubled, heart that I must let the events run their course and that without knowledge of Anna I would be completely lost and without a reason left to me to be alive on this earth, there would be nothing left on this side of death which may bring me comfort.

CHAPTER 29

The ladies nursing care

"Quickly, get help." Lucille called out to Frances, who had heard the commotion and came up from the basement kitchen to see the master bleeding in the hallway. Instinctively Frances hurried to the salon room above where she knew Anna was reading to improve her knowledge of the French language, she knew that in the absence of a physician that sweet gentle Anna would be the best option to help with nursing or medical care. The three ladies were soon helping Klebert to the main bedroom where they removed his blood-stained coat and soaked shirt. Anna asked for water and towels to wash away excess blood in order to view the wound more clearly and then apply sufficient pressure to bring the bleeding to a stop. Klebert was told to lie on his back, which he found difficult through the sharp piercing pain of the injury and the effects of excess alcohol from the long period of debauched drinking. It was evident that he'd involuntarily urinated whilst lying on the bed, a fact that Anna loudly brought to the attention of the other two ladies who had mixed emotions towards Klebert of mainly pity and sorrow but secretly with a tinge of enjoyment when witnessing his embarrassing distress. They were after all shared lover's of this man and therefore despite some feelings of anger towards him they also had some tenderness and sentimental emotions of sorrow that Klebert certainly didn't deserve. Anna had the experience of nursing the wounded before in both Ireland and England, she reminded Frances of this fact once again and as she did requested Lucille to bring the sewing kit, the gash was twelve inches in length but by good fortune hadn't penetrated the heart or cut badly into the rib cage. Klebert was very lucky indeed.

Anna had come to the rescue of her kidnapper and decided with him being in a weakened state to continue her psychological attack, she very audibly spoke to Lucille and Frances and beckoned them closer to view the wound.

"If I push here, I can break this main rib bone, then punch through applying full weight on this side. It will kill him in less than five minutes!" Something in her tone, now so familiar to the ladies of the house and Saumur, disclosed the fact that she wasn't serious but it was sufficient to put fear in Klebert who shook his head, despite being unable to speak his eyes pleaded for help.

"We need him alive," Frances spoke first, "he's got to put things right!"

"If he lives, this is the last time he'll sleep in this bed." Lucille added to Klebert's broken state of manhood as Anna began to treat the wound, she pierced two holes in a large towel and placed it around the torso of Klebert, then placed the handle of a hair brush through the holes and turned the handle clockwise tightly, this caused an outburst of loud anguish and pain from Klebert which brought a smile to Anna's face. After a short while the bleeding slowed and Anna started to suture the open gash. Having finished, a tight padding was applied and knotted with a cord from the curtain, Klebert was told to lie still and drink plenty of water by the ladies who left the room feeling more empowered than ever towards the man who'd brought so much misery to Anna and displeasure to the other ladies.

"I think we can use his weakness now dear friends, he's a

weak man, a pathetic excuse of manhood, he won't be banging on bedroom doors for a long while. We can drug him into submission and make his life a misery or I can pretend to warm to his character for my return home. Ladies, we have the advantage!" Anna laughed as they entered the salon. "Did you see anyone else in the doorway Lucille? Was there any sign of who attacked Klebert?"

"Not that I saw. No." Lucille answered without emotion.

◆ ◆ ◆

I lived in the shadows, sleeping outside Saumur during the afternoons when the streets were deserted as locals rested in their lodgings and houses and when my presence on the streets would be most noticed. I spent the evenings and most of the night until early hours opposite the house of Klebert and his kind family member or friend Lucille. I was able to sit on the cobbles about fifty yards away where visibility was sufficient for me to see anyone enter or leave the house but without my being detected. Unfortunately, despite occasionally seeing Lucille and another lady coming and going I still was unable to determine whether Anna was within the house. I considered whether I ought to change my viewing routine but Saumur was very crowded and lively during the morning and late afternoon, during these hours I needed to be amongst the bustling market place where I was inconspicuous with the other beggars. The best place to hide a needle is amongst a lot of other needles and not a haystack I thought, the residential street where Klebert lived was definitely not the place to go unnoticed and so this limited the time I could spend there observing.

At times I wondered whether Klebert was dead from his wounds, and if so why shouldn't I simply barge my way through the front door and find out once and for all if Anna was there. I was resolved to do this on many occasions but for one reason or another I held back, perhaps realising that any drastic action would prevent an easy escape. An escape that may need planning, perhaps with Anna and with the gold coins still in my possession maybe along with Anna's language skills then there was a faint chance of success! However I realised I would need to do something soon as my physical strength and willpower grew weaker with each passing hour.

My daily routine was to leave Klebert's street with an aching body from my rough nights sleep on the cobblestones wrapped, against the cold, in my heavy coat. In the morning when the church bell rang at four I would make my way to the river to wash and then settle in the market square where the drinking fountains, the scraps of bread and fruit, that had either fallen or been discarded were on the ground and made a poor but very needed breakfast. I'd watch the traders set up their stalls and see the now familiar faces of domestic servants come down for the morning household provisions. I thought at some point I would be bound to recognise the friendly faces of Lucille and her friend, the kind ladies who'd given me the very shirt on my back probably once owned by the odious Klebert, but there was no sign today.

As I sat with my head bowed, occasionally looking about me for the ladies, my dirty fingernails came into sharp focus and with them the large red K laundry mark. My mind wandered, how could I have sunk to this level of wretchedness and despair? It occurred to me that the only men I'd encountered in France of worth were the kind monk in the service of God and the innocent and decent kindly farmer, an occupation that I once shared before my stupidity. Would that I were there once more, on my farm with loved ones and how I envied the French farmer whose lifestyle was now lost to me. Again, and this time in pain, I looked at the red K mark that haunted and teased my senses, how pitiful a man I was to be wearing a shirt owned by my nemesis who'd killed my son and stolen my guilty love from me! I was sorely tempted to rip off the offending garment were it not for my being in need and so the K added salt into my open wounded heart!

How could I have missed the ladies yet again over these past few days I wondered, perhaps this morning would be the day, perhaps I'd see them and be led to Anna? No! Another morning without success. As the market cleared and my fellow beggars made their way to charitable hostels and doss houses I walked alone to the peaceful outskirts of Saumur where a field was my afternoon bed. After a few hours of rest and as the evening darkness began to set in, it was back to Klebert's street for another night's cold and depressing lookout.

CHAPTER 30

Klebert makes a recovery

Four days had passed since Klebert's fight and Anna decided it was best to remove the stitches in his chest wound through fear of infection setting in; the twice daily task of cleaning the wound was becoming an annoyance to whichever lady had drawn the shortest straw and undertaken the task. Anna was often asked to assist through her previous knowledge of nursing which became a topic often discussed as Klebert was treated.

"How often did you suture wounds like mine?" Klebert asked whilst wincing from the pressure being applied to his chest.

"Often in Ireland during our protests against the English landowners, they put down any decent or objections to anyone who opposed them. They didn't do it themselves, they used desperate and criminal types to leave the people living in misery, they were horrible criminals like you Klebert!" Anna stared at Klebert at this point, forcing him to look away to the wall in embarrassment. Once she'd finished removing the stitches and with a final wipe of the wound she left the room, as she did she gave the now familiar smile to Lucille and Frances who understood its meaning well, that her verbal attack on Klebert was another sign in belittling his resistance to the ladies dominance in all household matters.

"I need to talk to you Lucille, please stay a while, you too Frances," Klebert asked with a slight shortness of breath. "We're returning to England, there's another raid planned at the end of November. I need to be ready to go, you won't need me here and I need money for you all. If I'm killed in England you'll be taken care of by the 'tontine' scheme that the comrades have and will distribute funds should I be killed, so I might as well go."

Lucille spoke sternly and with coldness, she recalled the last departure of her husband which was a more affectionate occasion where she had a small degree of warmth towards him and concern for his safe return, mostly for ongoing economic security. However this time Lucille's attitude was of indifference as to Kleberts actions and return, if he died Anna had shown that she could manage the house very well in his absence albeit with a great deal of hard work.
"You must do as you wish!" Lucille said smiling at Frances.

Returning to the salon where Anna was reading Rousseau, the ladies discussed Klebert's news of a further raid.
"November, another raid to England. Do you think Klebert will be fit enough to go?" Frances asked Anna, who by now had dropped her book, showing interest at the prospect of returning to her daughters.
"If he'll take me back then he's certainly fit enough! What's the best plan to persuade him? Will you help me?" Anna excitedly asked. The ladies clearly wanted Anna to be happy and the only way for this to happen would be a return and therefore the three ladies sat on chairs facing each other frantically racking their brains to work out a plan of action. It was Frances who spoke first after a few minutes of thought.
"You need to give him hope! You need to concoct a believable story which shouldn't be too difficult for you." Frances giggled at the prospect of Klebert falling for an Anna lie; she believed Anna's stories were well aimed at gullible men and a useful tool in a women's armoury. In truth and despite the obvious affection

towards the Irish guest, Frances wasn't sure of any truth concerning Anna's history or her uplifting stories. "Tell him you were forced by, what did you call him, Albert? To leave your family in Ireland. Tell him that you'll be his 'friend' if he'll take you to England, collect your daughters and then settle down for a life in Ireland!"

"It's a brilliant plan, thank you Frances. He's so stupid, he's bound to fall for it." Anna gratefully smiled with laughter at Frances' suggestion.

"You're a dark horse with hidden depths", said Lucille, smiling at Frances, who joined in the laughter but coldly then added to the plan. "If you get back to England and your daughters it will be wonderful, but please alert the English authorities to his presence! I don't want him returning here, it's difficult for me to explain but if he takes you and leaves me then it's a final act of betrayal towards me. I'll be pleased for you to be home where you belong though." Lucille gave a knowing look whilst gesturing her comments towards Anna. "It would be wonderful to see you return here and maybe with your daughters one day. You'll always be welcome." Anna was acutely aware of the weakness of the male sex and understood very well Lucille's position, she had endured Kleberts infidelity on so many occasions with the act of lovemaking towards other women but never a complete desertion by her husband to another woman. It was the last straw, there would be no way back in Lucille's mind for Klebert, so evident that she'd be content to see him dead at English hands. 'Hell hath no fury!'

"Thank you, tomorrow I'll start being nice to him and spin him a yarn, give him some good old 'Irish blarney', I'll have him begging to take me back and then once there I'll betray him to the militia, I know a kind man who'll help me." For the first time since arriving in France Anna felt there was a good chance of a successful return, the three ladies spent the evening discussing Anna's homecoming and how her daughters would be so thrilled.

Anna entered Klebert's bedroom with morning coffee that she placed on the side table in front of the street window.

"You'll be in pain for a while but you can move around now, no sudden moves or bending down. It will take some time but you should make a good recovery." Klebert looked at Anna with his obvious sign of pathetic desperate yearning affection, like a docile dog, and was heartened by her presence without Lucille or Frances. This was the first opportunity he had to enter into personal conversation with Anna for some time, he'd become accustomed to accepting that he would never have any appeal towards her and therefore was confused to see her attending to him with more sympathetic affection and alone!

"Why have you brought my coffee? Yesterday you called me a 'criminal', I'm not sure why you'd do anything kind to me. It was true what you said, I am a criminal and I feel terrible for what I have done to you." Klebert fought back tears, tears of sincere grief, tears of anxiety of depression and guilt.

"I shall never understand why you took me, it was cruel. You clearly aren't a rapist without morals, you seem to have genuine remorse, I suspect if we'd met under different circumstances you and I would have got on well. Can you explain why you took me?" Anna was at her masterful best, knowing exactly what to say and at the right moment, with the right expression and bodily movements that were undetectable to all but the object of her persuasion.

"I can't honestly say, there was something about you that captivated me, something that was in your face and manner, your demeanour! I can't say why, only that it was a dreadful mistake." At this point, with a gasp of breath and painful sadness Klebert wept deeply.

"Well, I lied to you and I'm sorry also. I told you I was in England having fled Ireland for my protection and that I fled the English, British, rule. The truth is that I was part of that tyranny or at least my family were, but they were also cruel to me and arranged by force my marriage to a man named Albert who was bribed into taking me to England. However, just before you took me, I was notified that my family had been killed in a tragic accident. I was about to return to Ireland with my daughters, leaving my idle husband Albert behind, where I could live happily in the family home with the surrounding farm estates for our income and living. If I can get back to Ireland via England on route I'll be very rich. I still need you to help me get home and maybe in time we can forget all about my French trip and my being kidnapped!" Anna's blue eyes portrayed the required amount of helplessness, imploring and yet with excitable affection to make Klebert's heart flutter, his stomach filled with butterflies and hopefulness. "If we can get to Ireland it will be the answer to our prayers, green fields, freshwater lakes full of Rainbow Trout and in time I can forgive you. I can see you are a good person, you didn't rape me. We can become friends first and then in time we might be together, my husband doesn't exist to me, he's an irrelevance !" Anna didn't need to say anymore, Klebert was completely fooled, he was a fool, and Anna wondered how far he could be pushed into embarrassing himself further if it were not for her need to get home on the Aquilon ship that would be leaving soon. "If you are due to return to England soon could you take me? If you can, once we arrive on the south coast of England I know a hiding place until your comrades have left. We can then collect Mary and Sarah and then make our way home, my home, our home!" Anna smiled leaving the room and returned to the salon to impart her good news to Lucille such was her confidence that Klebert would agree to her clever trickery.

The front door slammed closed and Frances entered the salon with a large grin on her face and joined the ladies, she was informed of the good news that Klebert had been fooled by the initial stages of the plan and there was a strong degree of confidence that Klebert would take Anna home. Frances smiled and still in a breathless excitable mood from her rushing home she imparted her news.

"I've been talking to the ladies in the market and apparently Klebert's good friend 'David' is dead, found brutally beaten with a sword wound across his chest and it happened on the same night as Klebert was outside the door here pleading for assistance. Either Klebert killed David in a fight or they were both attacked by others!"
Anna leapt to her feet in delight.
"Wonderful, I have him, he can't, but help me return now for fear I'll blackmail him by letting it be known he killed David!" Anna's whole face lit up in ecstasy and she was joined by the other two ladies who formed a circle and danced around the salon with childlike giggling. "If, in the unlikely event he finds his way home after my return, which he won't, I'll make sure of it, you can blackmail him with the news of David's death. I saw him threaten to kill this man David on route here, on the wagon that brought us so it wasn't an attack by others on them, it was Klebert who murdered him! I'm sure of it. I intend to use this news to seal Klebert's fate, I'll speak with him again and without overtly stating that he'll be blackmailed I'll insinuate it, his only option will be to leave here once his murdering is discovered amongst his military comrades."

Anna excitedly left the room and ran up the flight of stairs to Klebert's bedroom and without the respect of a knock on the door rushed in.
"It's been reported that your friend 'David' is dead, he's been murdered, brutally beaten and killed with a sharp sword blade across his chest. He must have been attacked by the same man or group that attacked you!" Anna gave a look at this moment of such piercing inquisitiveness that Klebert was instantly showing his guilt, his face reddened with anguish and pain. He was caught in the moment and considered whether to continue the pretence of an attack on him and David by an unknown group and that being outnumbered there was no hope of repelling the violent mob but with his newfound honesty towards Anna he knew that he would be unable to give a

convincing lie.

"There was a man there and I'm sure he would have killed me as I came home wounded, I didn't recognise him but he called out my name, I wondered whether it was him that killed David and yet you are, I suspect correct that it was me who killed him. I didn't know he was dead for sure, I've been hoping that he survived but the truth is that it was me, we argued as we had done on the journey here that you witnessed, he wouldn't stop insinuating what I should do sexually to you. I realised how horrible a man he was, he raped a woman in the English drinking bar in the last raid and I'm sorry now to say that I killed a boy there. I want to change and be a better person, I've never raped a woman like he has!" Klebert looked away in sudden shock and fear that he'd let slip the news that he had done murder in Winchelsea, desperately he attempted to give an explanation having seen Anna's reaction. "It was a boy in the bar, he was protecting a woman from David, they were fighting when I entered the room so I obeyed my orders and killed him. I'm so sorry I did it now."

"What was the boy's name, who was the woman that David raped?" Anna secretly was fuming and outraged at this news, could it be someone that she had strong feelings for, could it be the son of a man she admired so much from afar! Her heart was wild with anger and she was sorely tempted to reach over to Klebert's wound and dig her fingers into the healing gash to bring her satisfaction and severe pain to the hapless quivering man before her. And yet in her masterful way she kept some calm and with two deep breaths was able to prevent showing her true feelings towards Klebert. She appreciated that an attack by her wouldn't bring her any closer to the English return she so craved and so spoke once more but this time with greater effort to hide her venom. "I suspect the woman David raped was Emma, she's the lady who works in the bar, she's truly a wonderful woman, she's so kind to everyone and even to my horrible husband who pesters her so much. I'm glad you killed David, he deserved to die but my advice is to let it be known you were attacked together by a mob if you are asked, the idea that it was one loan man who attacked and killed you both won't be believed by anyone. I don't think it will be very good for you if it's found out you killed David. Do you!" Anna's emphasis was on the final comment as she left the room with a very knowing and deliberate look that left no ambiguity. Klebert sheepishly nodded as he understood fully what had been said.

Anna returned to the salon in a saddened state, she knew Emma very well as a friend and valued lady from the Winchelsea community. She was now also full of anger as to Klebert's murderous actions and anxiously worried about who the boy could be from the pub; she was determined now more than ever that her kidnapper would be made to pay and suffer terribly. She was resolved to kill Klebert herself!

"I've let it be known that David is dead and he's confessed to the murdering. I said things will be very bad for him if it were discovered that he did the deed so I think it will aid our cause and he will take me home." Lucille, with mixed emotions of joy at the prospect of Klebert leaving but also sadness at Anna's departure, spoke first.

"I'll miss you, Anna but I understand you must return. We'll certainly manage well without him", Lucille gestured towards the upstairs master bedroom where Klebert sat whimpering on the bed. "We'll take in washing and maybe a lodger, perhaps passing priests on their way to Rome. We won't starve, will we Frances? Tomorrow morning if you go out for the morning bread Anna, I'll speak with Klebert giving him my blessings to take you back and be with you if that's what he wants, my endorsement will be sufficient enough to ensure he won't change his mind. When he's agreed I'll send him to you in the market with the good news."

CHAPTER 31

The day of decision

Klebert entered the salon having woken early in an excitable but troubled condition, he was heartened at the prospect of a renewed possibility of friendship with Anna but appreciated the huge challenge in front of him, he would need to show a great deal of repentance for his confession of the English boy's murder. He'd washed, shaved and then had breakfast in the dining room for the first time since his altercation with David. Klebert had had no knowledge of the outcome of his fight with David until Anna's breaking of the news, certainly he hadn't known for sure that David was dead, although he knew it was a possibility, he had wondered how severe his downward sweep of the sword was . He had dismissed it from his mind as of no interest, if David was dead then he deserved it, if he had been aided to recovery then so be it he would have learned his lesson. But on reflection with the evidence of his own wounds from the same evening's return from the bar and now the rumours likely to be spread by Anna and her newfound lady friends of Saumur, Klebert realised his position could be perilous. David wasn't overly popular amongst the militia but he was a member and appreciated as such, when men live and die in battle a perverse loyalty that breaks down the boundaries of morality and common decency come about.

Klebert knew for the first time that his days in Saumur were numbered, his only slight hesitancy and reluctance in leaving immediately, with Anna for Roscoff and the Aquilon, was now a slight tinge of moral responsibility towards his wife and for her future financial security. A woman deserted by a husband would be left vulnerable to other unscrupulous men to take advantage of her unprotected position. The Klebert of old with his selfish attitude and lacking a conscience would without hesitation have left his wife but now with a renewed sense of moral decency wanted to leave his wife on good terms.

Lucille was waiting for Klebert's arrival with her small speech at the ready, the very least that was necessary to see her wayward husband on his way, away from Saumur, away from France and secretly she hoped to see his death at the hand or request of Anna.

"I know how much you like Anna, I can see it so evidently in your behaviour, I understand as I like her also. I'd like her to stay here with us but she won't be happy and she won't make you happy either if you keep her here against her will. You must take her home, it's the right thing to do, it's the only thing to do and soon. Will you be able to take her on the next raid that you spoke of?"

Klebert, whilst still in pain from his chest wound, became overwhelmed with hope and relief at the prospect of a happy future. It was by no means a certainty as so many hurdles stood before him, but the first had been overcome with his wife's blessing in returning Anna, there would be no dispute or argument in his leaving once more. The second hurdle would be the Naval Officer's permission to allow Anna onto the Aquilon but this was virtually guaranteed as Klebert was the unofficial leader of the raiders and therefore had sway over any venture. The third hurdle was in Anna's hands as once on English soil she would hide him and then lead him from there to a brighter future. With tears welling in Klebert's eyes he thanked Lucille agreeing that he should make good his sins, his crime of kidnapping and this was his time for atonement and contrition.

"I'll put things right. I promise. Thank you Lucille, I don't deserve you and your kindness to me. I know I've been a bad husband, a bad human being, I won't stay in military service after I've returned Anna to her homeland and made amends!" Klebert stopped short of promising or saying he would return to her and Saumur. His real lack of guilt and contrition was very apparent in that he wouldn't admit to Lucille that his intentions were to abandon her forever, hoping for a life in Ireland.

"Well you can put things right with poor Anna, I can't say what it is about her but she's a special person and so it's important to do what's best for her. Please remind her once you've set her down on English soil that she's always welcome to return here again in better times. Anna's gone for the day's bread and provisions from the market. Why don't you get some fresh air for the first time since your injury and give her the good news, she really is a wonderful lady and will be so pleased to see her daughters again." Lucille played her part well, especially when considering that she knew her husband had no intention of a return. Klebert raised himself too quickly from his chair and with a wince of excitable anguish from his healing, but still smarting, wound was in pain. Klebert thanked his wife once more and smiled at Frances as he passed her in the hallway and left the house heading down the cobbled street towards the market place where the busy stalls were in full morning trade.

CHAPTER 32

Breaking point

Another night has passed as I drifted in and out of a sleeping stupor, I realised that anybody could have passed me by undetected and within feet of my presence. My drooping head and tramp like state had made me completely unrecognisable from my previous life as a clean shaven smart farmer. I believed that even had my wife Caroline passed me she wouldn't know me, such was my down and out condition. I lifted my aching body from the grass bank facing the Loire river, having washed my face, and upper body in the fresh cold water and considered my options once again. Should I bang on the front door of the Klebert house in the hope of finding Anna or should I give up and attempt a return to England with my gold? My weariness in body and mind made any rational thought virtually impossible. Should I give it one more day and night? Would I have the physical or mental capability left to attempt any of the above actions, how long did I have left before certain death would come not least because of the coming coldness of winter. A return to England I believed would mean my not returning to the Winchelsea home as I'd ruined my only chance of success with my treachery being discovered. I would need to find work and a new life in London, perhaps around the docks or a return to army service with a new identity especially if war is coming as Eclair and others all said and believed. These options gave me no encouragement, no belief in future happiness, it would be an existence without meaning, without incentive, and in deepest loss without Anna, Caroline or Tom. And yet it was Anna I was still in love with, a fantasy that was now becoming delusional as I grew weaker by the hour, desperate for hot food and a long sleep. In a weary and disoriented state I returned to my usual morning vigil at the marketplace in the hope that this might be the day Anna may appear to me. I was resolved to the decision that if she didn't appear today I would storm violently through the Klebert front door at nightfall.

The reality is I am here, rightly or wrongly, by mistake or design I must keep awake, alert to my last Saumur day of hope and chance. Would today bring me some better luck, a glimmer of hope, a chance to regain some mental energy as I took my place with the other beggars. We, the dishevelled down and outs, nodded in appreciation of each other's plight and ate the purposely thrown bread graciously given by the bakers who had set up their stalls from the carts that circled the market square. The morning sun rose above the church steeple giving a warming heat to my shivering bones and a red hue to the Saumur brickwork and glow over the river I'd just left which was down the slope on my left hand side. How I yearned each morning for this warmth, each morning I was rejuvenated by a small degree with the rising sun to a renewed sense of comfort and glimpse of what could be, but I knew I was on borrowed time!

I was aware of a fellow beggar becoming unusually interested in my presence and he affectionately attempted to start a conversation, on previous occasions he had avoided me but as I had become a regular sight to him it became clear that he may wish to form a friendship of fellow sufferers in adversity. I would have to move away and find another resting place but I was hesitant to do this and leave the best viewing position for my Anna. I smiled quickly and looked away from the man whose face began to frown with inquisitiveness. My hand reached for the envelope stating I was suffering mental illness from military service, how strange I thought that the first time I would need the letter of explanation since my begging of a meal from the farmhouse on route to Saumur would be to a lowly beggar and not someone in authority. The envelope lay beside the bag of gold coins and Livres, this would be my second option to free myself from the unwelcome stare of this vagrant whose gaze was now trancelike fixed in my direction, would a few gold coins make him go away, I grasped the bag in my inner pocket! By now the sun had risen so there were no shadows in the market and the red hue on the brickwork had been replaced by a sun that prevented full view without squinting at those passing by.

As I quickly looked around the stalls before me I made the decision to relocate my position as the beggar's stare was still annoyingly fixed on me, my view was suddenly and excitedly held by a woman walking on the other side of the marketplace where bread, cheese and meat stalls were located. At first there was a familiarity about her gate, her petite frame and the contours of her bottom and hips. My heart began to beat faster, it was the frame of a woman I'd admired so often from afar at home. She weaved in and out of my sight as the lady walked behind each stall and with each appearance I started to see the more familiar features, her blond hair neatly placed and combed back over her ears, her smooth and olive skin and full lips and her angelic face with the expression of kind innocence. My heart was now racing, it was her, my Anna, the object of my longing and affection for so long and the one I had come to save. What relief and joy to see her not just living but clearly thriving and blossoming in good health, she looked well and exactly how I remembered her.

Instinctively I knew what I would say, that Mary had sent me and then followed by the truth that I had come for her, that I would take her home, that I loved her and had for so long. I'd spent so long through moral duty, custom and fear of her rejection in not telling her of my love but that in her reported kidnapping I had given up everything in pursuit of love. I was now oblivious to the beggar on my right hand side approaching, I frantically winched myself up onto my aching feet using the hard stony wall behind to push myself up, I was dizzy with the speed of my rising up but once on my feet and standing I began to call out. All sense of my precarious position with false identity and in personal danger had gone from me as I called out. "Anna".

"Anna!" She hadn't heard, I was weak but attempted again but to no avail, "Anna" I shouted very loudly.

Then suddenly in fear I saw a man coming down from the street towards Anna, she as yet hadn't noticed him but I had and it was Klebert, the man responsible for Anna's taking and inadvertently the awful predicament I found myself in. I was held to the spot, petrified at the thought that he was approaching her and would inflict pain despite him being obviously wounded and walking with a cane. To my amazement he had a docile, grinning and almost lost in stupid love expression, a bizarre manner I thought from my last encounter where he was in a drunken fight with the dead man David. I was witnessing something very strange indeed.

For the fourth time and now in a blind panic I began to shout out to Anna but her gaze had now seen Klebert and she smiled at him! Not a smile of a forced captive but a smile of sincere delight in his arrival, a smile that deepened as the two drew nearer to each other. How was this happening, had I been duped, had Anna come to France willingly, had Mary known her mother had not been kidnapped, had the mother and daughter made a fool of me, had I lost my wife, family and farm in pursuit of madness that had led me and them, by association of my irresponsible stupidity, to ruin?

I watched the lovely Anna, the lady I had secretly obsessively adored and longed for from afar, loosely hug this dreadful man Klebert with what appeared to be some affectionate gratitude. I was overwhelmed with loss and despair, I felt an ache and sharp pain in my weak and frozen body. I stumbled back and felt the hard wall crash against me, I felt dizziness and pain, I was unable to shout anymore to Anna and as I began to fall my gold coins ripped free from my pocket and fell to the ground scattering and rolling across the sloping cobbles in all directions.

My frantic and gut wrenching lasting glimpse of Anna came as she and Klebert were, now standing in close proximity to each other, discussing what looked to be an imparting of cheery news. Their heads turned inquisitively in my direction at the commotion I had caused with the Saumur peasants desperately fighting in a frenzied scrum and scrambling for the falling coins. Did Anna recognise me? I wasn't sure, I think not, but did I see a flicker of recognition in her expression, was there an inquisitive movement in her frown and eyebrows of that sweet and beautiful face? Despite my disheveled and tramp-like appearance, would Anna see beyond my now lengthy greying and filthy beard, my drained ash like and tired face so aged over the previous few weeks? My final vision, before the hard impact felt as my head hit the cobblestone floor and unconsciousness, was of Anna's face, the face of my believed to be true love, the face that had turned me from a proud man to that of being responsible for my final and self inflicted demise, ruin and miserable end.

The End

Printed in Great Britain
by Amazon